I0664719

CARRY
ME
HOME

STERLING RIVERS

REAMSPINNER
PRESS

Published by
DREAMSPINNER PRESS

5032 Capital Circle SW, Suite 2, PMB# 279, Tallahassee, FL 32305-7886 USA
www.dreamspinnerpress.com

This is a work of fiction. Names, characters, places, and incidents either are the product of author imagination or are used fictitiously, and any resemblance to actual persons, living or dead, business establishments, events, or locales is entirely coincidental.

Carry Me Home
© 2016 Sterling Rivers.

Cover Art
© 2016 Resplendent Media, http://resplendentmedia.com/
Cover content is for illustrative purposes only and any person depicted on the cover is a model.

All rights reserved. This book is licensed to the original purchaser only. Duplication or distribution via any means is illegal and a violation of international copyright law, subject to criminal prosecution and upon conviction, fines, and/or imprisonment. Any eBook format cannot be legally loaned or given to others. No part of this book may be reproduced or transmitted in any form or by any means, electronic or mechanical, including photocopying, recording, or by any information storage and retrieval system, without the written permission of the Publisher, except where permitted by law. To request permission and all other inquiries, contact Dreamspinner Press, 5032 Capital Circle SW, Suite 2, PMB# 279, Tallahassee, FL 32305-7886, USA, or www.dreamspinnerpress.com.

ISBN: 978-1-63476-841-2
Digital ISBN: 978-1-63476-842-9
Library of Congress Control Number: 2015920895
Published February 2016
v. 1.0

Printed in the United States of America
∞

This paper meets the requirements of
ANSI/NISO Z39.48-1992 (Permanence of Paper).

CHAPTER ONE

As I passed the bend in the road, the landscape opened to reveal the house I'd grown up in. A few things had changed, most notably the rows and rows of corn that spanned the fields in the summer. I remembered hiding in them when I was a little boy, the stalks three times as tall as I was. My mother would chase me, pretending she couldn't find me. Now large sections of the crops had been replaced by giant windmills, their blades silently rotating in the moderate December breeze. Though I preferred the corn, I couldn't deny the wind machines were a marvel to look at. Mom had accepted an energy company's bid to build them on her land a few years ago, and the payout was decent, but she had told me quite adamantly it wasn't about the money.

I turned into the driveway, bypassing the "whale box," as I called it. It had been given to my father by a neighbor who liked to whittle logs into works of art. The actual mailbox was inside the whale's mouth, and the family name of Price spouted from its blowhole. I remembered thinking it was the coolest thing as a kid. *We don't have a mailbox, we have a whale box!*

I almost stopped to see if my little toy car was still buried behind it but kept going.

I pulled up to the front porch of the farmhouse and cut the engine, then rested my head against the seat. I wasn't ready for this, and I sure as hell didn't want to do it alone. But my sister was busy with her husband and new baby, and my father wasn't due to arrive in town until tomorrow morning. So it was up to me. As much as I wanted to avoid the whole thing, I knew a small part of me needed to covet this moment.

After my father had divorced Mom, and Missy went off to college, it had been just Mom and me. I knew my sister would ravage Mom's wardrobe for the best clothes and jewelry. My father would just trash everything, and no way was I hiring some removal service to desecrate her home.

Be a big boy, Aiden. I heard her encouraging words in my head as if she were sitting next to me. Twenty-nine years on this earth hadn't prepared me for what I knew I needed to do. It was my responsibility to get this done. Mom could count on me to sort through everything with care.

I stepped out of my Hummer and shut the door, the pop loud to my ears. Several jays were darting around the empty bird feeder and making a ruckus. It was nice to see the old oak that had been here since I could remember was still standing, the tire swing lulling back and forth from the wind that whistled softly as it blew through the leaves. I listened for the hum of the mills but got nothing. The rose bushes lining the front of the porch had grown wild, and the deck was littered with dead leaves. For a brief moment, I considered sweeping the porch—Mom would never allow such disarray.

I was aware I was stalling. With a lump stuck in my throat, I climbed the porch stairs and pushed the key into the lock. My hands were shaky, and it took several tries, but eventually I got the door open. The first step was the hardest. The interior of the house was quiet, the silence broken only by the rhythmic tick-tick of the cuckoo clock. The farmhouse smelled much like I remembered— flowers, herbs… love and cold nights warmed by the fireplace while nursing a mug of hot cocoa. But a crawling chill lingered, as if something were missing.

As I made my way to the kitchen, I kept my eyes in front of me, unable to look at the handmade furniture Mom liked to collect. Recalling the times she had taken me to the craft shows was just too painful right now. I was raw and vulnerable, and I hated it. It made me feel like a child rather than a twenty-nine-year-old man.

I yanked the fridge open and made a face as a blast of sour air hit me. I managed to locate a bottle of water and gulped it down until my stomach sloshed with fullness. Crushing the plastic in my palm, I sneered at the rotten fruit and spoiled lunch meat. My throat tightened as I snatched the half-full trash can from the pantry and began shoveling the decaying contents into it. I figured the fridge was as good a place as any to start, and the kitchen would smell better once it was clean. After all the food was trashed, I pulled out the shelves and set them in the sink, then started scrubbing the fridge. I had just finished rinsing everything when the funeral home called my cell. I let it go to voice mail.

I tried working through the beep of my phone, but I couldn't ignore it any longer. I listened to the message. I almost expected them to tell me there had been a mistake and Mom was fine, just needed a ride home.

"Mr. Price? This is Thomas Pinski with Model Funeral Home. I just want to assure you that everything is ready for tomorrow. Please, if you have any questions or concerns, don't hesitate to call us. We are here for you."

Not bothering to call them back, I deleted the recording. I didn't need another reminder that Mom was gone. Self-delusion had quickly become my best friend, and oddly, it was helping me cope. The idea this was just a horrible nightmare and the hospital had made a mistake kept the tears away. I had missed Mom something awful when I'd gone off to college, and her recent absence evoked that feeling. I almost believed I'd see her again. I told myself I would. I had to if I wanted to get through this.

I needed to believe the lie.

Working tirelessly to make the fridge sparkle, I put the shelves back, then moved to the freezer. I tossed everything, even the TV dinners that hadn't passed their expiration dates yet. Once I was done, I wiped down the outside, then straightened the magnets and snapshots. I took out the garbage and rinsed out the can in the backyard. By the time I'd finished, the sun was falling into the west, lighting up the clouds like fire. I took a moment to draw in a big breath. My sinuses were aching, not from allergies but from the tears I'd been holding back.

There was no time to mourn. I had to take care of the house.

I turned the can upside down so the water would drain, then headed back inside. After washing my hands, I returned to the front room and fisted my hair, unsure of what to do next. Mom had left the house and property to me, and I knew I was going to have to part with some of her belongings. But getting rid of anything nearly shattered me. I figured I could have a yard sale, but as I ran my eyes over the furniture and knickknacks, my heart refused to let anything go. Maybe I could just store it in the garage until I was ready?

I headed upstairs and found Missy's old room. It was barren, with the exception of a neatly made bed that probably hadn't been used since she'd left for college. Besides a dresser and discarded stuffed animals, the room was sterile, so I moved on. I passed my bedroom, deciding it would be the last thing I tackled. Doing a quick check of the upstairs bathroom, I found that nothing had changed. I knew the clunky duck toilet-paper dispenser would be staying. My father had complained when we brought it home from the craft fair, but Mom had loved it.

I found myself in front of Mom's room. It had once been my parents' bedroom, but when my father moved out, his belongings had gone with him. I recalled Mom trying to cope with the divorce by painting the room in pastels and trimming it with floral motifs. I'd helped her, and we ended up covered in paint. That year after my father left, I'd seen a lot of change. The plain eggshell-white walls of the living room turned pale purple. The cabinets were stripped of fine china and filled with awards Missy and I had won in school and artwork I'd created. Even at nine, I kind of understood Mom was trying to move on just as my father had, and crafts were her way of dealing with the emptiness his absence left.

I stared at the pale peach door for a good ten minutes, debating on whether to leave it for last or tackle the emotions that slumbered in her room. I berated myself for being such a nancy. I gripped the cold knob and put all my strength into turning it, but my muscles went limp. I pulled away and turned on my heel, deciding to leave it for last. It was as if my brain had been tossed in a blender turned on high. I had no idea where to start, what to keep or get rid of. The frustration made me want to cry, and I cursed as I burst out the front door. Angry and hurt, I kept walking, needing a distraction… anything.

By the time I got to the whale box, I felt calmer, the tension in my forehead easing a little. I blew out a big breath and traced the grooves in the wood with my fingers. On a whim, I grabbed my cell from my pocket and dialed Missy's number. It went to voice mail. No surprise, but it was nice to hear her voice no matter how clipped it sounded. I didn't bother to leave a message. I'd see her in the morning and ask her to help me with Mom's room after the funeral. I figured she knew more about women's fashion than I did. Besides, having her plunder Mom's stuff would help me clear the house sooner, and I could use the incentive.

I chuckled as I realized it would be the first time I'd talked to Missy in three years. She'd never kept in contact with me after she had graduated college, and I was lucky if I got a Christmas card from her. Missy had always been that way. Mom said she took after our father—restless, always on the lookout for the opportunity for something better.

I pushed those thoughts away and flipped the mailbox open to find stacks of letters shoved in so tightly, I had to tug them out with force. While I was sitting at Mom's bedside waiting for her to wake up, I never thought about picking up mail or managing the house. Everything had just sort of… stopped.

As I flipped through the mail, I found the postcard I'd sent from New York a few months back. She never had a chance to see it. Every time I traveled to a new city, I made sure to send her a souvenir. She had always wanted to travel but never got the opportunity, and I thought I could bring a little piece of the world to her instead.

I gathered the mail in my hands and headed back toward the house. I took a seat on the couch and began sorting through the jumble. I made quick work of the junk mail, tossing it into the trash, and when I was done, ended up with a large pile of bills. I bypassed the electric and gas and centered on the hospital invoices. I pinched the bridge of my nose as I read through them. Most were in past-due mode; others were threatening to take her to collections. I immediately got on the phone and was surprised that a majority of the billing departments were still open.

I wasn't sure why, but clearing her name made me feel better, and by the time I got done negotiating with the department that handled the paramedic's bill, it was dark outside, the crickets out in full force. I managed to set up payment arrangements with them and made a two-hundred-dollar "good-faith" payment right away. I wasn't sure how I was going to pay everything off. Mom's insurance had covered a good chunk of the costs, but there were thousands of dollars still owed. Part of that was my fault. I'd battled with Missy to keep life support on even though the doctors warned me there was no hope she'd come out of it. Last week I'd been convinced Mom was going to wake up and get better.

Strange how things changed so quickly. Then again, I still believed she was coming home.

I set aside some magazines. I'd call them tomorrow to cancel the subscriptions. Most of the essentials like electric and gas were paid up months in advance, so I put them on the back burner. After locating an empty box, I began sorting through papers and books, filling it with *Women's Health* and the like. I managed to find more boxes and marked them with *yard sale*, *trash*, and *storage*. By the time I was done going through the living room, I had filled three storage boxes with knickknacks. The other two were pretty much empty. I pinched my eyes closed in frustration. I felt like a hoarder, unable to let go of anything. Even the magazines were looking at me as if I had abandoned them.

I sighed. It was going to be a long night.

CHAPTER TWO

I MANAGED to grab about two hours of sleep during the night. My mind had been too occupied dealing with everything to settle down, and all I could think about was how to tackle the issue of organizing the house. After the attempt to straighten the clutter failed, I moved out into the garage and found a little more success there. Some of the junk belonged to my father—tools and such— so I gathered the last reminder that he had once lived here into a pile and made room for storage. I wondered if Mom had hung on to the tools for practical reasons or had been unable to completely let go of their life. I moved some of the "storage" boxes in and found several more boxes to put to use. After attempting to sort through Mom's stuff, with most of it ending up in the storage boxes again, I gave up and crashed in my old bed. It took me a long while to fall asleep, and when I awoke, it was only 3:00 a.m.

I decided to stay up and made some coffee. I watched the rising sun slowly illuminate the sky, the room brightening as the day got on its way, and listened as the first birds woke. It looked like the beginning of a nice day, so I opened a few windows, the cool morning air rushing in. It was welcome, and for the first time in months, I felt peaceful. I loved it here. There was a sort of untouched beauty I couldn't find in the city, and mornings like this made me wish I had never left. *I should have visited more*, I told myself. Maybe I could have taken Mom with me to New York. She would have loved that.

Unfortunately, the peace was quickly gone, shattered by the realization of what the day would bring.

When the cuckoo clock let me know it was six, I went upstairs to take a shower. I was dusty and sweaty, and I wanted to look my best. The water was scalding, but I liked it like that.

When I was done, I wiped the condensation away from the mirror and looked at my reflection. Jesus, I was a mess. Lack of sleep had really played on me.

I sighed heavily. My eyes were so like my mother's, it almost hurt to look at them. *As deep as the ocean*, she had said. *As green as emeralds.* I had her strawberry-blond hair too, which had made me the brunt of dumb-blond jokes from my ex-boyfriend. I didn't mind, though, as some had been funny. *Brian.* I had forgotten to tell him about Mom. We'd broken up years ago, so I didn't think he would care, but Mom had always been sweet to him. We had stayed in touch. Of course, she'd been under the impression we were just college buddies. But he was busy with his own life now, miles away from Texas. Besides, the last I'd heard he had a new boyfriend, and I doubted he had the time to deal with my drama.

After finishing up in the bathroom, I went downstairs in nothing but a towel wrapped around my waist. I had forgotten to drag my luggage in the night before. I silently apologized to Mom for running outside half-naked and retrieved my suitcase. I imagined her chastising me by using my full name, her arms folded over her chest. It made me smile. When I was six, I hadn't wanted to take a bath so badly that I fled, bare-assed naked. She had to chase me down the driveway and drag me back. My father had thought it was hilarious.

Things hadn't always been bad between my parents. My earliest memory was of them together, dancing in a warm spring breeze while I sat on a picnic cloth making a mess of a piece of apple pie. I thought back to when everything had changed for them, but it seemed more of a process rather than a snap—little things here and there, and then he was just… gone. Missy was going off to college, and it was just me and Mom. Then it was time for me to start my own life… and Mom was alone. I wondered if her tears at the airport were more for her loneliness rather than my growing up and leaving home.

I riffled through my luggage until I found my slacks and dress shirt. Nothing fancy, just traditional funeral gear, black dress pants and a black shirt. It was the nicest set of clothes I owned—Valentino, in fact—and had cost me a week's salary. It took me thirty minutes to get ready, and by the time I was headed out the door, I looked like the businessman I was. Not too bad, actually. Mom's Irish heritage combined with my father's strong bone structure had done me well.

I made sure everything was locked up, then headed down the road in my Hummer. I phoned Missy, but she didn't pick up. I guessed she was already there or on the way. I didn't bother calling my father and figured I would just see him there. We had drifted apart after my parents' divorce, his contact even scarcer than my sister's. I understood her absence, but I had come to resent him for not keeping in touch with me. Just because he no longer loved Mom, didn't mean I stopped being his son.

When I got to the funeral home, it was a quarter after seven. The service didn't begin until eight, but there were several people I recognized standing around in the main hall, friends of Mom and my cousin, Allie, with her six-year-old son, Justin. The director met me instantly, and I accepted his hand. His voice was full of compassion as he welcomed me and told me not to hesitate to ask if I needed anything.

I simply thanked him.

"Aiden," Allie said in a hushed tone as she hugged me. I'll never understand why people thought they needed to be quiet at funerals, as if they were afraid they might wake the dead. After the silence last night, I could have used a little noise, and I thought Mom could have too.

I accepted my cousin's hug, not completely comfortable with the attention.

"I'm so sorry," she said against my neck.

"Thanks." I put forth my best effort to be polite, but I wanted my space. She didn't give it to me, holding on as if she needed the support more than I did. Allie had always been in my life and had probably seen more of Mom in the past few years than my sister. She had been bedside a lot too, offering me a cup of coffee every now and then as I waited for Mom to wake up, but she had had to go back to Oklahoma to deal with her own life.

"I just can't believe this is happening." Allie sniffed and pulled away. "I mean, she was so young. Healthy…."

I'd heard this all before, and frankly, I was tired of it. Like Mom's age had something to do with someone's driving? As if the woman might have decided not to get in the car fall-down drunk because Mom was in good health? I knew I was being an ass, but I couldn't help it, so I let Allie mourn, nodding in agreement. After all, I was more of a listener than a talker.

She backed away. "Justin, come say hello to Uncky Aiden."

The little boy had been sitting by the stairs and burst into action, crashing into me with a big hug. I returned the gesture and ruffled his hair. I hadn't seen the kid since he was a toddler and was surprised at how big he'd gotten.

"Mom, I have to pee," he said, dancing.

Allie dried her tears and gave me another hug, then took Justin to find the bathroom. When I was alone, I turned to the front door and waited. I kept my eyes in front of me, unable to look at the parlor where Mom rested. I could see the white folding chairs and pedestals topped with extravagant floral arrangements out of the corners of my eyes. That had been one thing I was adamant about. Mom had loved gardening, and I didn't hesitate to splurge on the flowers. I could see the red carpet leading up to where her casket was. It was open, and I was sure I could make out her shape. I kept my gaze straight ahead. If that wasn't Mom, then this wasn't happening.

"Aiden?"

It took me a moment to realize someone was trying to get my attention before I instinctively threw my hand out. A tall black man I didn't know accepted it and greeted me, a soft smile on his face, but his eyes looked haunted, as if he'd gone days without sleep. He was around my mother's age and dressed in a nice pair of slacks and a fine shirt. He seemed vaguely familiar, but I couldn't quite place him.

"I am Darnell, a friend of your mother," he said. "I recognized you from your picture."

"Oh," I muttered.

A look of uneasy disappointment crossed his face, and I knew he'd totally gotten the wrong impression from my reaction… or lack of. I had little energy to correct his assumption, though I understood his position. Growing up, I'd noticed things about my father that I didn't particularly like. It wasn't until I was in high school that I realized he didn't approve of black people, and that was putting it gently. I was sure Darnell felt out of place here, and strangely, it made me like the guy, though I had no idea who he was.

Darnell seemed to think an explanation was in order. "I'm with West-Prairie Energy and helped set up the deal with your mother."

I nodded, conceding it made sense. I replied robotically, "It's nice to meet you."

"Likewise. She was a remarkable woman." He must have sensed my disinterest in any sort of conversation because he floated into the parlor without another word.

More people arrived, and I accepted their condolences, forcing myself to be polite. All the "such a shame" remarks agitated me—as if I needed another reminder of how Mom had died. At ten to eight I checked my watch, wondering where Missy and my father could be. I figured they were caught in traffic or something. My sister finally arrived at two minutes before eight, looking stunning in a slimming black dress. Her lawyer husband was behind her, carrying my nephew in a rocker.

"Sis," I said meekly.

She offered me a quick hug and looked around, no doubt trying to find something to complain about. We had butted heads a few times, planning the funeral. She wanted to break the bank, but I had been more conservative. Yes, I wanted to give Mom a good send-off, but I knew she would have scolded me for spending money I didn't have. Despite my job paying well, I still had a lot of student loans to pay off. After a lot of bickering, Missy and I finally came to a resolution. I let her plan the dinner as long as she stayed within a reasonable budget. Looking at the gleaming diamond on her finger now, I should have let her go all out.

"Traffic was ridiculous. How are you?"

"Okay," I lied and turned my attention to her husband. "Scott, nice to see you again."

"Likewise." The guy nodded. I really didn't know much about Missy's husband, other than he was twice her age and some sort of criminal defense attorney out of Los Angeles. Apparently they'd met on a trip her senior year of college and had fallen in love.

Making a face that could curdle milk, Missy asked, "Are those folding chairs?"

Scott sighed. "Don't start, Melissa."

She didn't pay attention to him and walked into the room to inspect everything, I assumed. I minded my own business as Scott rolled his eyes, following her. My sister had never been an easy person to get along with, and I couldn't help wondering how long it would be before she called me, crying that Scott was leaving her. I knew it was a shit thing to think about my sister, but my emotions were all over the place and anger made me feel a little better. It was easier to examine other people's failings than my own.

I should have visited Mom more.

My father finally arrived five minutes later and looking older than I remembered but well kept. He'd always had that rich air about him. My grandfather on my dad's side had said Dad had married down. I had never liked the old man, but I liked to think Dad married up with Mom.

"Aiden," he said, and we shook hands.

It was strange. I didn't want any more attention and condolences, but I suddenly craved a hug from my father. Sadly, he seemed to be doing just fine.

"You left me, David," a woman said in a hushed voice as she rushed to join Dad.

He chuckled. "Are you going to tell me you couldn't find the front door?"

I hadn't recognized her at first. My attention had been on my father, but I knew who she was the instant she started talking about Dad's lack of empathy. This was Carol, his new wife. As they bickered softly, something inside me uncurled. I couldn't believe he'd brought her here. Why would she even want to come? I knew Dad had moved on long ago, but…. Mom and Dad had been married for years and had two kids together. Surely he still cared about her? Why would he disrespect her memory like this? It was like he was intentionally flaunting his hot young wife in front of Mom.

I parted my lips to speak, but she laughed behind her hand, stealing my resolve. I didn't want to do or say something I'd regret later, no matter how pleased he seemed with her taunting. She tucked her arm in his, and they walked into the room where Mom rested without saying anything else to me. *This is my mother's goddamned funeral!* I had to shout it in my head. I'd never met Carol before, but I instantly disliked her. Not for her age, which I guessed was half my father's own, but her callous disregard for the situation.

"I can't believe he brought her." Missy came up next to me, but she seemed amused by the whole thing. When I didn't say anything, she remarked simply, "The pastor is starting soon."

I nodded and she left. I needed a few minutes to calm down. I wanted to give my father a piece of my mind but refused to make a scene at Mom's funeral. I was quaking inside, and I wasn't sure if the tears lodged in my head were from sorrow or frustration. The anger was quickly replaced by dread. I couldn't hide any longer. I had to go in there and watch the pastor talk about Mom and listen as people tried to hide their sobs. And I would have to see Mom lying there, her body stiff, her skin pale and painted with makeup to make it look like she was sleeping.

This could be the last time I got to see her.

Could be? This *was* the last time I'd ever see her. As I took tentative steps toward the parlor, my denial was shattered by the reality of the situation. *Mom is gone.* Her brain had been so damaged in the car accident that life support had been the only thing keeping her alive. And after five weeks of waiting and praying to a God I'd never believed in, I finally found the courage to pull the plug. The woman that had always been there for me was gone…. She was never coming back.

Mom is dead.

My throat tightened as I entered the room. I managed to reach the back row of chairs before I took my seat, my legs crumbling. I felt as if my head was going to explode, and my stomach hurt even though I hadn't eaten for a day. I zoned out as people came up to speak about Mom. I heard them talking, but I had no idea what was said. All I could see was her casket surrounded by lovely flowers I had debated over, her pale form lying motionless.

When people started to turn toward me I blinked, confused as to why everyone was looking at me. Had I made an undignified noise?

"Aiden?" the pastor asked softly. "Did you want to come up and speak?"

I bit my lip and got up on shaky feet, my legs feeling numb as I made my way over to the podium. I wanted to hide behind it but managed to dig out a piece of notebook paper I had scribbled on. I was surprised to find it was blank and frowned in confusion. I had sat down the other day to write a eulogy—maybe I had grabbed the wrong paper?

"Mom—" My brain was unable to connect the words to my mouth, but what could I say that hadn't already been said? Everyone here knew she had been an amazing person, kind and joyous, so what else could I possibly say? I tried speaking, but nothing would come out. I could feel everyone's eyes on me, waiting, heads darting around in search of an explanation.

Get with the fucking program, I chastised myself.

I cleared my throat and balled the blank piece of paper in my hand, then stepped down. Soft whispers floated around me as I returned to my seat, but I had officially checked out. My body grew light, and my mind drifted to a place where none of this was real.

If I had taken Mom to New York with me, she'd be alive today.

CHAPTER THREE

WHEN I awoke the next day, it was 10:00 a.m. It took me a moment to realize I'd slept nearly twelve hours, but I still felt exhausted. I wanted to roll over and go back to sleep, but that wasn't very productive, so I forced myself out of bed and downstairs.

I got the coffee going, figuring I was going to need it. As I stood at the window sipping my drink, I felt as if time had gone backward. Yesterday hadn't really happened, and Mom was still asleep in the hospital. The dinner last night was hazy. I could hardly remember what had transpired or what I'd eaten. It felt more like a social outing than a funeral dinner, but that was Missy for you.

I watched the clouds floating in the sky as if they held the answer to what I was supposed to do now. The last few days I had been occupied planning the funeral and sorting Mom's house, but one was done and the other seemed impossible to accomplish. I wasn't sure how long I stood there, staring out into the world as if it were a two-dimensional television rather than a real live breathing thing. The chirps of dozens of birds eventually pulled me from my trance, and I watched as they fluttered around the bird feeder.

Something was injected into my system, and I found the will to do something other than phase out. I left the house and headed straight for the shed where Mom kept the gardening supplies and found what I was looking for. I filled the bird feeder to the top with fresh seed, then went around to the front porch. The birds immediately descended, snatching seeds and squawking with joy.

A sense of accomplishment engulfed me. Mom had loved animals, birds in particular, and I couldn't recall a day that feeder was ever empty. I silently apologized to her for neglecting to refill it yesterday. A squirrel watched from the oak tree, flicking its tail as if it wanted in on the action. I made a mental note to pick up some peanuts from the store. I needed to go shopping, as the fridge was bare bones.

I retrieved the broom and started sweeping the porch, pushing away weeks of dirt and debris. When that was done, I collected the leaves into a pile and scooped them into a bag. The porch light ended up needing to be changed too. I spent a good hour trying to track down a new bulb to no avail and eventually ended up in the attic. Mom used to chastise me for crawling up there when I was a kid, so I'd forgotten about it. She had said it was dusty and cold and no place for a little boy. I hadn't remembered there being this much stuff up here, though. Some of it was furniture she'd bought from the craft fair, but the rest looked antique. I bit my lip as I pulled a sheet off a large bureau, the craftsmanship top-notch. Maybe this was why she hadn't wanted me to play up here. I couldn't help wondering if there was any value in it.

I scavenged through the drawers, not finding much. I discovered a big trunk of men's clothes—fancy suits and shiny dress shoes. Some of it was rather nice, classic but elegant. I found several more trunks, some with women's clothes, others filled with fine china wrapped in newspaper. While it was exciting to discover all this old junk, it was just more for me to do.

I ran my hand through my hair, trying to figure out what to do. All the furniture and clothes must have belonged to my grandparents on Mom's side, leftover relics from the past Mom had held on to. Grandma had died when I was two, Granddad several years earlier. I didn't remember her, but Mom had pictures of her holding me when I was a baby. If Mom had kept the mementos all this time, then they had sentimental value to her, which meant I was never going to be able to get rid of them. I sighed, frustrated. I knew I needed help.

I phoned Missy first and left her a voice mail, letting her know I had found some expensive-looking clothes. If I could get her here, then I could try and guilt her into helping me clean out the house. I called my father next and left a message for him too. I was kind of glad he didn't pick up. I was still angry with him.

Having no luck getting in touch with my family, I plopped my ass on a chest and slouched. This was harder than I ever thought it would be. *It's just fucking stuff*, I told myself. I could put my mother in the ground without shedding a tear, so why was I having such a hard time letting go of her things? I phoned Missy again. When it went to voice mail, I didn't bother leaving a message.

I wasn't sure how long I moped in the attic, but as the sun dipped into the west, the glaring light hit me in the eye. It was as if Mom was yelling at me, telling me to wake up and get with it. I knew I was reaching, but I dialed Brian's number.

I was dumped to voice mail, and I was both relieved and disappointed. "Hey…. It's me. Ah, I know you're probably busy, but I could use some human contact. Shit…. That didn't come out right. That's not what I meant—I mean if you want to… no strings. Never mind. Anyway, Mom died. I buried her yesterday. I'm sorry I didn't tell you, but I know you're doing your own thing. Listen, I'm at her house if you want to stop by sometime. Just a couple of beers and a movie or more if you want. Just—"

The beep cut me off, letting me know I'd gone past my limit. I almost called again just to finish the message but decided I sounded desperate enough for one day. I knew I was being a needy bitch, but I hoped I didn't cause him problems. I hadn't meant to imply sex, but what was done, was done.

Sitting in the attic and sulking wasn't going to do me any good, so I put everything back in its place. When I snapped the sheet to cover the bureau, I noticed a chest in a corner I had missed before. It was metal and military green. I had wasted enough time pouting up here, but I couldn't help it. I opened it and found stacks of old, yellowed letters and a small wooden box. Inside was a black-and-white photo of a man I didn't know and a Medal of Honor.

"George Walter McMurray," I whispered to myself, tracing his face. Huh. I thought this was my great-uncle, Georgie. Mom had mentioned him once or twice. Apparently he had died in Vietnam when Mom was a baby.

I glanced at the letters and tracked the postage stamps. They spanned the late fifties to the early sixties and were from someone called "Bibby." There were a lot, at least a hundred, but I put them back, refusing to get distracted. I needed to get it together and do what needed to be done.

When I got back downstairs, I realized I had lost a lot of the day. It was nearly five, and on cue, my stomach reminded me it was dinnertime. I ordered a pizza, not feeling like going out. As I waited for the food to arrive, I managed to clean up some random Christmas decorations and move them out into the garage. I phoned Missy again, which went straight to voice mail. I tried Dad—no answer. I figured I'd try them again in the morning.

THE NEXT morning, I managed to get up early. When I checked my phone, I was disappointed to find that neither Missy nor Dad had returned my calls. It was still early, so I figured they'd get to me when they got up. Missy was a new mom after all, and I had been a handful when I was a kid, so I didn't fault her absence. I also left a message for my boss, updating him on the situation and when I could return to work. My job had been understanding these past few weeks, but I knew I was pushing it.

I warmed up some leftover pizza. I wasn't really all that hungry but ate nonetheless. After a quick shower and cup of coffee, I found myself back in the attic. I had reasoned that all this old stuff wasn't actually Mom's, so it would be the easiest to let go of. I thought about phoning some antique shops and seeing if they wanted anything but was quickly drawn to my mysterious uncle's belongings. I fiddled with the medal for a while, trying to imagine how he'd gotten it. Had it been presented to a wife or my grandmother upon his death?

I set it aside and picked up the stash of letters. I counted one hundred and fourteen over a five-year period. Bibby must have been my uncle's wife or girlfriend, but Mom had never mentioned her. Then again, she'd only been a few years old when he had died. I had never been interested in family history before, but my curiosity sparked.

The letters were arranged in order, so I plucked the first one. There was something very honest and romantic about it. In an age of technology, no one wrote longhand like this anymore. I tried to imagine the thought that had gone into it, the expression on Bibby's face as she put her emotions on paper.

My Dearest Georgie,

You have only been gone a few days now, but already I miss you deeply. You don't know how hard it was to let you go, to watch as the train disappeared into the distance. This ache in my chest won't go away, and I fear it will always be there until you return safe and whole to me. I thought about what you said the other day. In fact, it's all I've thought about these past few days. You're right, but you know I'm a hopeless romantic. I'm going to wait, and though the days will be long and the nights cold, I'm going to wait for you to come back. I refuse to think about the ramifications of our relationship. Instead, I choose to focus on what brought us together. When I am alone, I will think about the day you return. When I sleep, I will dream about our life together.

Yours Always,
Bibby

My Dearest Georgie,

I know I'm writing again so soon, but I miss you. I've replayed the day you left in my head so many times, I can remember the smallest of details.

*That fussy child in the courtyard, the warm breeze
blowing in from the south, the soft scent of lavender
on the wind. The breakfast we shared and when you
spilled coffee all over your trousers. It makes me
smile when I remember the way you looked at me,
as if I was the most important person in your life. I
could see the hope in your eyes, hope that everything
would be okay, that you will come home.*

*Here you were going off to war, while I was the
one needing the support. As far as farewells go, it
was perfect. But there is one thing I regret. I wished
I had kissed you on the platform. I wish I had thrown
caution to the wind and pulled you against me.
Ignored the looks and the whispers. I think that flush
on your cheeks would have been wonderful. When
you come back to me, I promise I will kiss you no
matter who may see. I won't hesitate to put my arm
around you at the passion pit or share a soda with
you at the diner. After all, this town could use a little
scandal, don't you think?*

*Yours Always,
Bibby*

I refolded the letters carefully. So Uncky Georgie had a boo.
I snickered to myself. Still, the tone was laced with so much love
that it made my chest ache. I couldn't imagine watching the man I
loved leaving to go off to war, knowing he might never return. Then
again, with Mom being gone, I felt as if I could relate to Bibby's
pain. I vaguely wondered if she was still alive. Had she remarried?
Had kids? Did she ever think about what her life might have been
like had my uncle come back? And why did it seem like they had
to keep their relationship a secret? Retrieving an envelope, I ran
a finger across the name of Alice Barrington listed on the return
address. Maybe I was just reading too much into it.

Too emotionally distraught to continue, I put the letters away and went back downstairs. I was too raw to deal with the pain of missing someone. Besides, things needed to be done. No more crying over furniture and knickknacks. I needed to act like an adult. Yes, it was hard, but it had to be done. Mom wouldn't want me to sit here and rot.

I yanked open the front door to head into town for supplies, only to stop in my tracks.

"Why didn't you tell me? I would have been here for you," Brian said, his nostrils flaring.

"Brian... what—?"

He pulled open the screen and stepped in, his chocolate eyes intense. "I got your call. I was in Nevada, so I left right away."

I pinched the bridge of my nose. This was what I had wanted to avoid. And it was so like him. He'd always been a little impulsive. "I know you're busy. I didn't want to interfere—"

He didn't give me a chance to finish, just pulled me into a crushing hug. I didn't fight him. As always, he was solid and warm, and at the moment I was willing to accept any contact. I wasn't sure when the shift from leave-me-alone to need-lotsa-hugs had occurred, but I was glad someone was here. The house instantly felt warmer, the deafening silence not so alarming.

"You bastard, you know me better than that," he chided good-naturedly and backed away.

I could do nothing but look at him. He was handsome if not a little hawkish. I tried to remember when things had gone south for us, but all I could think about was how glad I was that he was here. "I didn't create any trouble, did I? That was not my intention. It's just that there's so much to do and no one to help."

He made a face at me. "Trouble?"

"Your boyfriend?"

Chuckling, he tipped his head back. "Oh, that. Let's just say it was more of a 'few beers and a movie' kind of thing."

I blushed. "I hadn't meant to imply—"

"Yeah, you did." He winked, then looked around. "And it's okay, really. Times likes these make us weird."

"I'd offer you something to drink, but all I have is bottled water," I said, leading him into the kitchen. I looked inside the fridge anyway, as if somehow little elves had restocked it with alcohol. "I do have leftover pizza, though."

"You should have told me, Aiden."

I stood up straight and took a deep breath. "I wanted to, but I couldn't seem to get the words out."

He whispered a curse. "I'm sorry. Can I ask…?"

I knew what he was inquiring about. Brian had visited Mom in the hospital once but had to go back to Houston for work.

"I pulled the plug." I didn't look at him, but I could see out the corner of my eye that he didn't know what to say. And I didn't want him to broach that subject. I was surprised I had managed to even say it.

"Well, I'm here now. I've got a little free time, so let me help. If you just want to hang out, that's cool. I just want you to know I'm here for you."

I dragged my eyes to him. Now I remembered…. It wasn't that we were a bad match. In fact, we had a lot in common, but life had set us on different paths. We were from two different worlds, and he was due to fill a position in Europe in a few months, so after college we had decided not to go through the down and outs of long-distance degeneration. We had started as friends and intended to remain that way.

I managed a smile. "Thanks."

He nodded, appeased. "That pizza still on the table?"

I couldn't help but beam. "Yeah, I'll zap it for you."

Brian laughed and took a seat at the kitchen table. "Just like college." As I tossed the pizza in the microwave, he remarked, "Wow, everything is still the same."

"Yeah. Lots of stuff to organize. I can't seem to get much done." A long minute of silence passed, and I watched the plate of pizza slowly turn inside the microwave.

"Maybe you shouldn't be in such a hurry to get it all packed up," he suggested as I set his food on the table.

I shrugged. "I don't know. I feel as if I need to do something, not just sit here on my ass and sulk."

"You're supposed to mourn." He smiled softly.

"Yeah, I guess. So how are things for you? It's been a while since we last talked," I started, needing to change the subject.

"Great! Everything has been confirmed. I can't wait. I'm so excited."

"I'm happy for you," I said honestly.

He tipped his head, his eyes brightening. "You know, if you didn't have your own life going for you, I'd ask you to come with."

The thought of leaving everything behind and joining Brian in Europe was appealing. What was left of my family hardly ever spoke to me, so what did I have here anyway? It was a nice dream. I chuckled. "Yeah. Maybe I'll come visit every now and then."

I watched as Brian bit into his pizza and chewed quietly, his eyes on me. They were thoughtful, searching, and I knew he was wondering if I was okay. Was I? I had to ask myself that question. As much as I wanted to deny it, I was torn by my mother's death. I hadn't even accepted it yet. So was I okay?

Brian's eyes narrowed on me. "Tell you what. Time here is limited for me, and I bet you could use a pick-me-up. What do you say we hit the town, get a few drinks?"

I beamed, the smile splitting my face. "That sounds good."

His tongue running across his bottom lip, Brian did a once-over on me. "Were you serious about the beer and a movie?"

I chuckled salaciously. "It was a slip of the tongue, but I am now."

He nodded, pushing his half-eaten pizza away. "No strings."

"None."

That naughty little smirk I was familiar with appeared, and my jeans got tight as the prospect of hot, raunchy sex loomed. I needed it more than I realized. I needed the distraction, and I couldn't think of a better person than Brian to share it with.

As we sat there feeling each other up with our eyes, I found my voice. "Feel like skipping the foreplay?"

Chuckling, he rose to his feet fluidly, and I took his hand, leading him up the stairs to my old bedroom. I closed the door behind us, then pressed him against it. I didn't hesitate to bridge the distance between our lips. He let me control the kiss, and I set a slow but thorough pace, his hands cupping my ass, fingers digging into the denim.

I whispered against his lips, "I need you to fuck me."

He nodded. Throughout our relationship I had been happy playing the top, but every now and then I needed to feel a dick in my ass. Needed to experience that loss of control, the absence of power. Right now I wanted someone else to do the grunt work and make the decisions.

Brian undid my pants and gripped my cock. I gasped into his mouth as he fondled me while his other hand skimmed my crack. He broke away long enough to mutter, "You need it hard, don't you?"

His erotic words left me breathless, and I nodded. Next thing I knew I was being thrown on the bed. I sputtered a laugh as he helped me out of my pants, then removed his shirt. When we were both naked, he covered me with his body, our cocks meeting. It felt so good to have a warm body against mine, that I—

The door suddenly opened, my father appearing like a phantom. I had time enough to see the horror cross his face before he slammed it shut. As crude curse words were hissed out in the hall, Brian and I scrambled to get dressed. Anger crawled up my throat like bad heartburn. Of all the times my father had decided to show up, it had to be now?

"Shit," Brian whispered harshly, but there was amusement in his voice. "Guess it's pointless to climb out the window."

I looked at him, feeling numb again.

"Aiden, goddamn it! What the fuck!" my father growled from behind the door.

Brian looked at me uneasily, and I blurted, "He didn't know."

He did a fish impression for a moment. "I thought you told them."

I looked away, unable to meet his eyes. "I lied."

The implications must have hit him, because he muttered another "Shit" and forced his socks on. I suddenly felt like a little boy caught doing something I shouldn't and wanted to do anything to avoid going out there and explaining to my father what he had just seen. I remembered thinking when I was a kid how much more fun life would be when I was grown up. Now I just wanted to hide in my room like a child.

"Do you... want me to sneak out the window?" Brian asked pensively.

Damn him, but I was going to miss him when he left for Europe.

"No, that's silly. Besides, it's my house. Mom left it to me," I said, feeling a little quarrelsome with my father. I knew how this was going to turn out, but I didn't want to drag Brian into my drama, so I nodded and he followed.

My heart was hammering, and my cheeks burned as I led him down the stairs. Dad was in the kitchen venting to Carol. I couldn't believe she was here. Why had he even told her? I urged Brian out the front door none too gently. I didn't want him to hear what I was about to say.

"Aiden, I have to go back in the morning, but I have some free time coming up in a few weeks before I head to Europe. We can do something then. I meant what I said earlier—I'm here for you. Promise me you'll call me if you need anything."

"I promise," I lied.

He nodded, giving me one last, longing glance before he hopped in his car and left. I knew he was a little disappointed I had lied about telling my parents I was gay, but I also knew he understood why I'd done it. His coming out hadn't been the easiest thing in the world, either.

As his car disappeared down the road, anger suffused me. I supposed it had been building up over time, but I was determined to play this out civilly. I went back in and found my father in the kitchen pulling his hair while Carol leaned against the counter, her arms folded over her ample chest.

"Dad," I said, and when his attention shot to me, I followed it up with, "I'm gay."

He blinked at me as if he was having trouble comprehending. He looked to Carol, who didn't say anything, then back to me. "Did Audrey know?"

At the mention of Mom, something stabbed me in the chest. I shook my head. I felt that him speaking her name did her an injustice.

"Jesus fucking Christ," he growled and scrubbed his face. "You've got a lot of nerve bringing this filth into her house."

Laughter bubbled up. "You are one to talk."

He looked at me, his eyes burning with fury. Hell, I wanted it, but I wasn't sure why. Carol attempted to soothe him, but he was having none of that. As she tried to reason with him, I felt bad about insulting her to her face. Truth was, I really didn't know her.

"Why are you here?" I prompted my father.

"Because you keep filling up my inbox!" he snapped, as if trying to communicate with him was an annoyance. "Damn it, no son of mine is a faggot."

"Right." I sighed. "Except that I am your son and I am a faggot."

I'd heard it all before—*queer, homo, fairy*. I'd grown immune to the words, but hearing one come from my father's mouth took something from me I knew I'd never get back. What if I had told Mom? Would she have thought the same thing—not out loud but internally? I could handle my father disapproving, after all he was more of an acquaintance than anything, but Mom?

My sinuses started to ache again, and I thought my head would explode. "Well, this is my house now, and I'm going to do whatever I want in it, and that includes fucking men, so if you don't like it, you can leave. You've never given a damn before, so please don't start now."

My father was furious beyond words, the blood pooling in his face. He seemed to have no idea how to respond. He simply grabbed Carol by the arm and stormed out. "You're lucky she died before she found out!"

As the screen door slammed behind him, something deep in my chest cavity exploded, the shrapnel shredding my soul. Even though his words hurt me, I wanted my father, my dad, to hug me and tell me he loved me just like he had when I was a little boy. I wanted to know why he had left me and Missy without a second thought. I wanted him to confirm that he was proud of me following in his footsteps and getting a good job.

No surprise, I knew I had expected too much from him.

"You have some tools sitting in the garage. I'd appreciate it if you'd collect them," I said numbly as my father stormed off.

CHAPTER FOUR

MY HEAD was pounding as I slowly came awake. The birds outside sounded loud, their whistles shrill, and I winced as I forced my eyes open. Much of last night was a haze. After the fight with my father, I couldn't stand the loneliness anymore, so I went down to a bar, the first I could find, and got smashed.

I could recall some cops giving me a ride home. Guess I'd gotten thrown out, but hell, at least I had the common sense not to drive home. Or maybe the bartender had been smart enough to call the good ole boys in blue to get me home? In which case, I didn't want to think what I might have done had I been left to my own devices. I'd always considered myself responsible, but in my current frame of mind, I had no idea what I was capable of. And the irony of that situation nearly bowled me over in laughter.

How easy it was to judge other people's mistakes.

I rolled over and groaned. Something was inside my head chirping and making an annoyance of itself. It took me a moment to realize my cell phone was determined to inform me I had missed calls. I didn't need to look at the screen to know who it was, and I sure as hell didn't feel like listening to my father insult me again, so I dragged myself into the bathroom and took a much-needed piss.

Washing my hands, I blinked at my reflection, not recognizing the person in the mirror. I looked worse than before, older, as if I'd aged ten years. I could still hear my father's words in my mind as if he were whispering into my ear. What a disappointment I must be to him.

I tossed down some aspirin and returned to my room. I plopped on my stomach, too exhausted to do much else. I considered going for round two at the bar, but the Hummer was still parked in town. I was going to have to pick it up eventually, but an unavailable ride meant I didn't have a way to the bar. I'd never gotten drunk before, not so much that I couldn't remember anything, and it scared me. Grandpa on my dad's side had always favored the bottle, and he was the type of drunk that was prone to mean words and actions. I'd only witnessed it a few times, but it was enough.

And I sure as fuck didn't want to be the person that ran over someone's mother.

I snatched my phone, shocked to realize it was four in the afternoon. Not only that, but Missy had called twice. I listened to her first message, real shock in her voice as she detailed what my father had told her and wanted to know if it was true. Her second message was a lot harsher, and I deleted it. Brian had called too, wanting to see if I was okay. I was desperate to hear his voice, but I refused to lay all this shit on him.

Fuck my father and sister. They hadn't given a shit about me or my mother for years, so why the hell did they care who I screwed? Anger reared its sleepy head, and I was tempted to call my father to tell him what a shitty parent he had been, then let Missy know what I thought about her richer-than-thou attitude, but I managed to refrain.

The effects of the alcohol subsided, and I wanted to cry. I had no one to turn to now, no one to hug me tight and tell me everything would be okay… that they loved me. I felt empty, lifeless. It wasn't just Mom being gone, but I never got the chance to tell her who I really was. Deep down, I was sure she would have accepted me, taken Brian in a big hug, and welcomed him into our little family.

I mourned for the lost opportunity, the regret piling up on me like a mudslide.

"I'm gay," I mumbled, imagining she was sitting next to me.

I love you, Aiden. I heard her voice in my mind.

As the pressure in my head rebuilt, I forced myself out of bed and down the stairs, needing to take my mind off everything. But all the furniture and silly knickknacks reminded me of Mom. I had nowhere to go, nowhere to hide. I wasn't ready to say good-bye, and I didn't know how to deal with that.

I had a hard time catching my breath as I crawled up into the attic and closed the door behind me. I sat there for a long while, trying to push back the tears that were building in my head. As I focused on the sound of moving air through my body, the tension in my head eased. When I opened my eyes, my gaze fell on the military footlocker nestled in the corner.

On shaky limbs, I came to sit next to the chest and popped it open. The stack of letters was waiting for me. I admired the coarseness of the paper in my hands for a while, then plucked the next letter in the pile. Bibby talked about how much she missed Georgie but was determined to hold on to the hope he would come home. She mentioned a friend that had just found out her husband had been killed and couldn't imagine the pain the woman was experiencing.

As I read through more, my frown flip-flopped at some jokes Bibby told Georgie she'd heard recently. Some were rather crude, others stupid. Bibby seemed to write every week, sometimes twice, and as Bibby's correspondence turned lighter and more hopeful, I thought how brave Bibby must have been to know that at any moment someone could come knocking on her door to tell her Georgie had been killed.

The pile of letters I'd read through started to grow, and I found an old shoebox to set them in. It was dark outside, the crickets yammering, the moon slowly cresting. I went back downstairs and warmed up some pizza. I gathered my food and a drink, along with a throw blanket, and climbed back into the attic. Getting nice and cozy, I let my bones settle. My cell phone went off several times downstairs, but I didn't bother answering.

I read more, wishing I could see Georgie's correspondence back. I'm sure he had a lot of tales to tell, fears and hopes to share from his time in the war. I thought about what his last letter might have said, what he thought about just before he died. I imagined he realized just how loved he was, and I prayed it had given him some small measure of peace. I lost track of time, my headache eventually dulling to a distant thump, but I couldn't stop reading.

My Dearest Georgie,

It's been one year since you left me. Sometimes it feels longer, other days less. Everything is blending together, and I don't recognize the town anymore. Without you it's become dull. I've heard rumors. Some people are saying the war is almost over, others tell me it's just starting. I don't know which to believe, but I hope for the former. Another woman in our town just lost her husband. Every time I see that army truck come down the road, I'm terrified it's going to stop at your mother's house. I'm so relieved when it keeps going. I'm sure my fear is nothing compared to what you're going through over there, but sometimes the pain is so much I can't breathe, and it feels as if my head is going to explode. Still, I refuse to let go of the hope that you will come back.

I apologize for being a downer. I know I promised I wouldn't dwell on your absence. So here is something different for you. Little Jack next door told me that he watched a movie in class informing them how to avoid homosexuals. I know it's not exactly what you might want to hear, but I thought it was quite funny. You've known me all my life; you know I don't give a flying fart what they think about us. No one is going to tell me I can't love you, not even you. Nothing can replace the moment we first made love, the way it felt to be connected to you in such a way. Nothing so wonderful should ever be wrong.

I think about it a lot when I'm lying in bed, cold and lonely, and it gets me through dark nights. I want you to know that you are not alone over there. I might not be there in body, but you have always

*had my heart. From the moment when I ran over you
with my bike, you had my heart.*

> *Forever Yours,*
> *Bibby*

I could barely read the text anymore, the letters blurring together. I didn't think my brain could process anything else either. I wiped the stuck tears from my eyes and read the letter over and over, trying to convince myself my brain was correctly interpreting the words.

Bibby was a *man*.

I caressed the paper with my thumb, lost in my thoughts. Was Alice Barrington a ruse to hide their relationship? Suddenly it didn't seem so out of place. No wonder they'd been so reserved. God, I couldn't imagine what they had gone through, needing to hide who they were, having to be careful no one noticed they were a little too close—the fear they must have experienced that their secret would get out. I couldn't help thinking about their time together, locked away from the rest of the world… just them and the love they held for each other.

I wasn't sure why, but my head loosened and the ache in my chest eased.

The sun rose as I read on, and I was unable to keep from laughing when Bibby told a silly joke or stop crying when he told Georgie how lonely he felt at night. It was as if I was a part of their inner circle, despite not knowing either of them. I felt privileged having been let in. I wanted to scream to all the naysayers and demand to know how they could think my uncle and Bibby's love was wrong.

I wondered if Mom had read Bibby's letters. It was a startling thought.

Something started hammering downstairs, and I stilled until I recognized my sister's voice calling my name, demanding I come out and explain myself.

What's to explain? Being gay wasn't something that required extensive study to comprehend.

With my car gone, she seemed to decide I wasn't home and took off, kicking up dust on her way out. I sighed and closed my eyes, wishing I could just float away to another place and time.

I must have fallen asleep, because I jerked awake. Little time seemed to have passed, the sun still high in the sky. Reluctantly, I put the letters away and went downstairs. I took a much-needed shower and grabbed some coffee. I deleted the six messages on my phone without listening. I wished I could be as brave as Bibby had been. I didn't doubt that if he'd lived in my time, he'd be out and proud.

I found myself dialing my father's number, and he picked up on the first ring.

"Aiden, Jesus Christ!" he growled. "Where have you been? I got a call from the sheriff to tell me they had to drive you home—"

"I got a little drunk," I interjected. Of course my little adventure would get back to my father, considering he and the sheriff were friends.

He was silent for a moment. "I wish you would have said something sooner so we could have gotten you help."

That familiar hot pressure in my chest returned. I knew what he was hinting at, and it pissed me off. "It's not something that needs fixing, Dad."

I held the phone away from my ear as he bitched, shouting colorful expletives. Funny, but he'd never been so vocal before. Maybe if he had been more communicative, he and Mom might have stayed married. I didn't bother responding, just cut the call. What was the point? He obviously didn't want an explanation and wasn't interested in understanding what I was going through. Never mind that, but this was not the time to debate my sexuality. It was the time to mourn for Mom. What a selfish bastard.

As my cell chimed, I thought about Mom. She had to have known about Uncle Georgie… read the letters. I recalled her spending time in the attic late at night, the soft glow of a candle letting me

34

know someone was up there. It nearly convinced me that she would have accepted my orientation, if only I had had the courage to tell her. And even if she didn't, she deserved to know the real me.

As my phone continued to ring, I scrubbed my face. Something needed to change. So my father and sister were homophobes—not all that surprising, really. That wasn't something I could control or change. Mom was gone, and I knew I had to stop moping around and accept that. Everyone died, and sons lost their mothers. But my biggest regret was that I hadn't given her the opportunity to really know who I was. Hell, I'd kind of followed what my father had wanted for my life. Majoring in business wasn't my dream job. It got the bills paid and set me for life, but it wasn't what I had wanted to do.

Something needs to change. My mother's death was the straw that had finally broken my back, and everything else was just frosting on the shit cake.

Something needed to change.

Wanting to let the tears flow but determined to hold them back, I stuffed clothes into a suitcase and loaded up a cooler with cold pizza and bottled water. I filled the bird feeder to the top, then ended up dumping the rest of the bag on the ground. I secured the barn and house, then hopped in the cab I had ordered with Georgie's footlocker tucked under my arm.

I watched as Mom's house got smaller, as if it were shrinking… disappearing.

Something needed to change.

Having the opportunity to examine my life, I realized I didn't have much of one. I could admit I had never really been happy since my father had left. Content but not happy. I needed to do this… needed to do something for *me*, and I couldn't think of anything better than meeting the man my uncle had loved.

Hell, some space from my rotten family might do me some good.

CHAPTER FIVE

MY EYES were pinching as I pulled into a little motel in Valley Forge, Montana—a not-so-small town at the base of the Rocky Mountains. From a quick Google expedition using the Wi-Fi at a fast-food joint, I had learned Valley Forge was one of the major farming communities in the county that specialized in livestock, particularly cattle. It was also a minor tourist attraction. More importantly, it was the town listed on the return address of Bibby's letters.

I had been tempted to stop hours ago, but I was so close to my destination that I forced myself to keep driving. Now that I'd made it, I wanted to collapse in a soft bed and sleep for two days straight. I nearly collapsed getting out of the car. I was weak, my legs like pudding, but I dragged myself into the motel lobby by sheer will. I had mulled over stopping several towns back for a good nap, but I knew if I did, I'd end up spending the night reading through Bibby's letters. At least on the road I was forced to pay attention to where I was going.

A plump woman in her midfifties greeted me with one of those Southern hospitality smiles. "What can I do for you, hon?"

"Single room, please. Can you charge me for two days? I'm not sure how long I'm staying," I said, attempting a pleasant expression, and pulled out my credit card. I hesitated, wondering if they even accepted—

The woman laughed. "We aren't *that* old-fashioned."

"Sorry." I blushed. "This is my first time in Montana."

She nodded. "We get a lot of your kind here."

I couldn't help it. I actually smiled. "Am I that out of my element?"

She stopped what she was doing and leaned forward, her baby blues narrowing on me. After a moment I wiggled and wondered if I'd said something wrong. She grinned and shook her finger at me.

"Country born but raised in the city…. Wait, don't tell me! College, then… I'm sensing… lawyer! No, wait. I see money, you around money."

I was agape, more so from her accuracy. "Close. I'm what I like to call an organizer. I go into a failing company and restructure. It's kind of boring, really."

I had to stop myself from admitting I pretty much uprooted companies and sold them off in parts for profit. I hated it, and it hadn't been my first choice, but the lure of good pay and benefits had been tempting. Unfortunately I hadn't realized what I was getting into when I applied for the job. I thought I would be helping these businesses, not exploiting their misfortunes.

She snapped her fingers in excitement, her cheeks rising. "I was dang close! My mother always said my sister had the gift, but I tell you I'm getting better every day."

I nodded, feeling chatty. "My mother was a farmer's daughter. Corn for livestock, mostly. I grew up on the farm but moved to California until I got my degree. Now I move around and go wherever my job wants to put me, but I've spent a lot of time in New York."

"Don't tell me!" she gasped and rubbed her temples. "Oklahoma?"

I chuckled. "Texas."

"Well, they are right next to each other. The general area, you know?" Her cheery disposition suddenly dropped, and her eyes narrowed on me. "You aren't from Weston Corp, are you?"

"Uh… no, ma'am," I stumbled, feeling uneasy under her shrewd gaze. "I'm here on personal business."

And just like that, I was back in her good graces. She snapped her fingers again and beamed, accepting my card. "Well, then! Welcome to Montana, hon! We got a little bit of everything and a lot a bit of heart, so I'm sure you'll find what you're looking for. I'm Gina, by the way, but you can call me Gigi."

I accepted my card back, feeling strangely light. "Aiden, and thanks."

"Since I like you so much, I'm going to give you my best room." She grinned and handed me a key. "I always run a clean business, but this one is the most charming of the lot. If you need anything, don't hesitate to ask."

"Will do, thanks again." I collected my belongings and made a move to turn but stilled. "You wouldn't by chance know an elderly gentleman that goes by the name of Bibby, would you?"

Gigi frowned and stroked her chin. "I can't recall that I do."

I nodded my thanks. I didn't think my inquiry would pan out, anyway. Things weren't that easy. Heck, I wasn't even sure if the guy was still alive, and if he was, he could have moved halfway around the globe. As Gigi turned around to go about her business, I suddenly realized how impulsive and silly my decision to travel several states away to track someone down was. Even Brian would have chastised me. Honestly, it felt good to do something different and unexpected, though. Something that didn't take a lot of contemplation and planning. At least I had an address, I mused.

I'd opened my mouth to ask if she might point me in the general direction of Orange Blossom Drive when the sound of bells cut me off.

Gigi squeaked and came around to hug the guy that walked in. "My goodness, Cody! Where have you been? I haven't seen you for days. Wait… are you wanting me to sign something? That's it, isn't it? That's why you're here."

The young man beamed, dimples creasing his cheeks. "The clipboard in my hand is a dead giveaway."

Gigi tsked. "I didn't even notice it. I really am getting better, you know."

His smile reached for his ears, and I took a second to do a discreet once-over on him. He was a contradiction in every way. He was dressed in a plaid shirt and classic blue jeans, but the pair of Converse All Stars didn't quite match his country getup. He had that homegrown, farm-boy countenance, gorgeous blue eyes and sandy locks, but the row of earrings slinking up his ear countered a ranching background. I allowed myself to leer for a moment.

"Surrrre…," he teased. "But you're right. I need your signature."

Gigi sighed but obliged him, accepting the clipboard. Too tired to wait around, I decided to crash and deal with the problem of locating the house in the morning. A quick search on Google Maps should set me in the right direction, and all I needed was a little luck that Bibby still lived there. I had just touched the door when the young man stopped me.

"You… sorry. Hello. I'm Cody." He smiled something beautiful and took my hand.

"Uh, hi," I managed, returning the gesture. He had a nice firm handshake, a sure sign of confidence, and his palm was remarkably smooth. "Aiden."

"Nice to meet you. My girl Gigi will take good care of you. Don't you worry." He leaned in and whispered, "She's not crazy, just super friendly. Mind if I steal a moment of your time? I just need your Hancock."

"Cody, don't harass my customers!" Gigi chided.

"I'm not harassing him," Cody replied, amusement in his tone. "I'm just making small talk."

"Do you remember what happened last time you made small talk with a guest?"

"He was a Republican," Cody reasoned, as if that explained everything.

As amused as I was by their banter, I really needed sleep, and judging from the man's attitude, I wasn't getting to my bed until I signed his petition. I didn't even bother to read it. I was all for demonstration and making oneself heard, but I was ready to collapse where I stood. I scribbled my name, then returned the clipboard to him.

"Thanks! You don't know how much your two seconds means," he said. He bit his lip before adding, "I hope I didn't offend you, by the way."

I was so out of it, all I could do was mutter a befuddled, "What?"

"Being a Republican, I mean." He smiled, his face lighting up. "If you are… which I don't think so, but it's cool."

I shook my head and shrugged, not sure what to say to that. I had little love for politics. The entire system was corrupt in my eyes.

"Cody," Gina admonished. "Can't you see the poor boy is exhausted? Let him get to his room."

Cody's eyes widened. "Wow, you do look like you're ready to fall over. Sorry, dude. But thank you. If you need anything, just ask. We're all pretty welcoming around here. Oh, and if you're looking for some comfort food, try Mama Hen's. The blueberry pie is the best. Oh, and the meatloaf—"

"Cody," Gina sighed.

Cody blinked at me, then apologized profusely. "I ramble sometimes. Anyway, welcome to our little slice of paradise."

He winked at me, then proceeded to hold the door open. I thanked him, and he gave me another one of those dazzling smiles. As I headed down to my room, I couldn't help fantasizing about the guy. If there was anything I could say about Montana, it was that the men were smoking. Chuckling at my strange frame of mind, I found my room and slid the key home. It took a little effort to get the door to budge, but when I was finally inside, I headed straight for the bed and collapsed. All I knew was the heaviness in my body and the soft, cool blankets under me.

My mind completely disconnected, and it was glorious.

I JERKED awake, pillows scattering every which way. It was light outside, illumination seeping through the ugly floral curtains. Blinking, I wiped away the crust from my eyes. My brows rose. I must have stumbled into some 1950s TV show. The decor was all cheesy vintage cottage, and for a moment I couldn't remember how I had gotten here.

As everything trickled back into my skull I stretched, growling at the wonderful sensation. I wasn't sure why I felt so good, but I wasn't going to question it. The sleep had done wonders, and I was reluctant to get out of bed but forced myself onto my feet. I located my cell and gaped. I had slept through the evening and all the way to morning. I hadn't realized how exhausted I'd been, but having caught up on my sleep, I felt rejuvenated.

I darted for the bathroom and relieved myself, then washed my face with the scented soap provided. I couldn't help shaking my head at the decor, but as Gigi promised, she ran a clean house. Realizing I had little to work with, I rushed to my car to retrieve my suitcase. My uncle's chest pulled at me, but I managed to ignore it. I wanted to avoid all temptation until I settled in. I had a hunch I was going to be here more than two days. There would be plenty of time to look through everything, but right now I needed a few hours to unwind. As I organized what few belongings I had brought, my stomach started complaining.

I dressed appropriately, glad I had the foresight to pack some winter-ready clothes. Stepping outside, I stilled, catching sight of the mountains looming in the distance like pale phantoms. They were breathtaking, humbling. Texas could be lovely, but this was a whole other world. Pulling the crisp, cool air deep into my lungs, I stepped into the motel's main office.

"Can I help you?" a young woman asked, stifling a yawn.

Feeling better than I had in days, I teased, "Long night?"

She snorted. "You have no idea. The nights just drag when you have so little to do."

I nodded, conceding the point. "I'm in One A. I was wondering if you could point me to Mama Hen's."

Her expression brightened, as if she were glad for the mental stimulation, and she perked up. I listened intently as she detailed directions and promptly thanked her. I retrieved my laptop from the room, then hopped in the Hummer and headed toward the restaurant. Mama Hen's was easy enough to find, but the parking lot was jam-packed. When I was seated at a table, I ordered a cup of coffee and was thrilled to find that the place offered Wi-Fi. Loading my coffee with sugar, I brought up MapQuest. I plugged in the return address on Bibby's letters and frowned as the results popped up. The house seemed to be smack in the middle of a strip mall. I double- and triple-checked, wondering if I had read the address wrong. It was handwritten, after all. I cursed myself for not bringing one of the envelopes with me.

When the waitress returned, I ordered pancakes with a side of sausage. "Would you by chance know where Orange Blossom Drive might be?" I inquired.

She gave me a quizzical look. "Sorry, I've only lived in Valley Forge for a few months."

I thanked her and proceeded to glare at the webpage. I was starting to feel really dumb for dropping everything and driving halfway across the country. I realized I'd put very little thought into this, but I was used to playing it safe, and doing something unexpected and careless was exciting. Still, I was left scratching my head on where to go from here.

When my breakfast arrived, I stashed my laptop and turned my attention on the food. I sighed as I ate, the fluffy pancakes exactly what I needed. Gazing out the window for a long while, I watched the people darting back and forth and the passing of the cars. I wondered what was happening back home. Did Missy or my father even know I was gone? I reckoned I should at least let them know I was alive and well. I filed that thought for a later date.

I requested the check and paid promptly, realizing I had no idea what to do next. I supposed I could drive to where the map indicated Orange Blossom Drive should be, but I wasn't in the mood to end up lost in an unfamiliar town.

"Come here often?"

It took me a second to realize someone was speaking to me, and as I looked up from my table, I gaped. The young man looking down at me was familiar, but his blinding beauty short-circuited my brain. All I could process were bright blue eyes and an infectious smile.

"Hey…," I managed, my throat parched.

"Cody," he finished, the corners of his eyes crinkling. "Good, huh?"

Good? More like great. When I realized he was referring to the food, I shook my head. "Ah, yeah. Thanks for recommending the place."

"No problem," he said, his eyes dipping down for an instant.

Heat coursed through my body, and not because I was dressed for winter. I cleared my throat, and asked, "Do you know the area well?"

He shrugged, his bulky plaid jacket bunching. "Not born but raised here. You looking for something in particular?"

The idea he might be able to help in my quest excited me more than I liked. I was willing to take whatever help I could get, though. Holding my hand out to the booth, I asked, "Would you like a cup of coffee?"

He seemed momentarily surprised but accepted my offer and slid into the seat opposite me. When he was settled, he arched his brows. "So what are you looking for?"

His question brought up all sorts of personal pondering. What was I looking for? I was aware what I had done wasn't exactly healthy, and if I were smart, I would go home and deal with my problems like a normal human being. I had a hard time finding my words, and I had no idea how to explain why I was here.

"Hey, Cody!"

He beamed and shot to his feet, then scooped the waitress up in a bear hug. I watched as she giggled, completely delighted, and I suddenly felt out of place. I got up to leave, but Cody stopped me.

"Wait, sorry," he said, catching his breath, looking as giddy as she was. "I'm a busy boy today, so many people to do and places to see. Why don't we meet tomorrow afternoon for lunch and I'll give you a tour? I'll help you find that thing you're looking for too."

I opened my mouth to respond, but nothing came out. He darted his intense eyes all over my face in search of an answer. Jesus, but this guy had a way of stealing my words. I nodded, intending to say something, but he cut me off.

"Awesome! One o'clock?"

"Okay," I mumbled.

His smile widened, and I was powerless to keep my own from splitting my face.

As I left Mama Hen's, I forced myself not to look back. I really needed to get laid, I thought. All this pent-up frustration wasn't doing me any good. Figuring I had little to do for the rest of the day, I returned to my motel room. As I pushed my way through the door, I could hear my cell letting me know I had several missed messages—four from my father and one from Missy and... a text from Brian.

My thumb hovered for a long moment, but I rang him, needing to hear his voice.

"I'm glad you called, Aiden. I was getting a little worried. Did you break your fingers moving furniture?" he asked, his tone even.

"Sorry," I apologized, feeling guilty for making him worry. "I just have a lot on my plate right now, and I didn't want you to get involved."

He was silent for a moment. "Do you consider me your friend? I mean, I know we were an item, and I suppose we can place ourselves firmly in the 'ex' category, but I like to think we are friends. What about you?"

Heat rushed to my face, and I looked down. He sounded hurt, and I mentally berated myself for being the direct cause of his pain. "Of course we are friends, Brian. I'm sorry I made you think otherwise."

He let out a heavy breath. "Are you okay? I mean really? I can't imagine this has been very easy for you—your mother and your father."

I couldn't respond right away. It was just another question I had no answer to. Was I okay? I wanted to lie and brush him off but settled for half-truths. "I'm coping."

"Aiden... I love you."

I heard the words, but it took a moment for them to sink in. I'd never heard that particular sentence from his lips before, even when we had been together, and it shook my foundation so hard I thought I'd collapse.

His laugh came through the phone like a purr. "Sorry. Let me rephrase that. We might not be together, but you were my first, and you will always be very dear to my heart. I need you to know I'm here if you need someone to talk to. Please tell me you understand."

It was strange, but his confession that he wasn't in love with me was a huge weight removed. Still, the idea that he cared enough to be concerned about me warmed my insides. I nodded, my voice a rasp. "Thank you."

He seemed satisfied, shifting our conversation over to his preparations to move to Europe. As I listened, I wanted to tell him how much I was going to miss him, but I refrained, not wanting to elicit emotions. He had no idea I was in Montana either. I could imagine he wouldn't be very impressed. As his stories came to a close, I wanted to confess everything to him, but I knew if I did, he would rush up here in an attempt to play hero.

"I meant what I said before. We're going to do something before I leave. Hell, you want to go to an amusement park and ride the coaster until we puke, I'm game," he said, his tone lighter.

I grinned, liking that idea. "I might have to take you up on that."

"Okay. We'll talk soon. Promise me you'll call if you're feeling down?"

It took a lot of effort to get the words out. "I promise."

We hung up, and I plopped my ass on the mussed bed. Running my fingers through my hair, I wanted to go back to Texas and make preparations to move to Europe with Brian. Neither of us had said it, but we both knew we would likely never see each other again. Something painful stabbed me in the heart with every beat, and my sinuses tightened. If I had stopped seeking my father's approval, I might have followed Brian's career choice. We could have been together all these years, preparing to move to Europe together. The things we might have seen and done....

I wanted to blame my father for every bad thing that had ever happened to me, for Missy drifting away, for me and Brian breaking up—for Mom's accident. I knew it was unfair, but I was bitter, and putting the fault on him was easy.

It was still light outside when I crawled under the blanket. I just wanted to hide from the whole world.

CHAPTER SIX

MY SLEEPING schedule had been thrown out of whack, and I spent most of the night watching old movies and guzzling soda from the machine down the hall. When morning came, I took a long, hot shower and headed down to a Dunkin' Donuts for some coffee. Now that it was nearly time to meet Cody at Mama Hen's, I was ready for a nap.

When I arrived at the diner, I was relieved to see it wasn't as busy. I parked the Hummer and took my time walking to the door, my stomach twisting. Of course it could have been the jelly donut I'd consumed. I knew I should have declined Cody's help. It wasn't that I was ungrateful, but I was in a weird mood, and he seemed like the sort of person that would do anything to try and turn that frown upside down... even if he didn't know me.

As soon as I entered, I spotted him. How could I miss the giant palm waving at me in the air? A flush crept up my neck. I ignored the looks of curiosity as several diners regarded me and headed toward the guy. His smile outshone the afternoon sun, and I thought I was going to need sunglasses while in his presence.

"How are you?" he asked a bit loudly.

"Okay. You?" I responded politely, taking my seat in the booth.

"Great! It's a nice day, isn't it?"

I shrugged. "I don't know. Is twenty degrees considered nice around here?"

My words sounded rude to my ears, and I hadn't meant to come off like a jerk. It was just hard to see the bright side when I had so many dark spots in my life hanging around. I had to remind myself that he didn't have to take the time to help me but he was, and I should show a little gratitude.

47

He laughed. "Well, yeah. I mean, its perfect cuddle weather, you know?"

"Hey, you two," a woman said, coming up with a coffeepot. I realized it was the same waitress who had served me breakfast yesterday.

"Hey, babe!" Cody beamed, and I thought he might shoot out of his seat.

After she filled his cup, she turned to me. "Nice to see you again."

I nodded cordially.

"This is… damn, I didn't get your name," Cody said, ruffling his hair.

"Aiden."

"Abby, this is Aiden." He grinned. "Aiden isn't from around here. In fact, I don't know why he's here, but I thought I would help him with that. I mean, the last time we got a drifter this time of the year, the guy ended up stranded in his car for two days on the side of the road."

As he went on with his story, I wanted to correct his assumption of me, but he wouldn't let me get a word in, detailing everything from how much snow had surrounded the car to the delirious state the man had been found in.

"Cody," Abby prompted.

"What?" He blinked at her, his cheeks mottling. "Oh, right. Sorry. I rambled. Anyway, are you off soon, Abs? Maybe you can help us. Three heads are better than two, and all that."

"Not for a few more hours." She pouted lipsticked lips. "I'll be right back, okay?"

When she was gone, I said, "You don't have to do this. I'm sure you'd rather spend time with your girlfriend than—"

He sputtered a laugh. "She isn't my girlfriend."

"Oh." It was all I could say, because I felt totally lost.

I watched blankly as he peeled open a straw, bent it in half, then stuck it in the corner of his mouth. "Gigi tells me you're from Texas?"

48

"Yeah."

"Never been. Not sure if I want to, but it's my goal in life to see every state at least once, so I guess I'll have to eventually, right? I'll leave it for last… no, second to last, because Hawaii, man… can't drive there."

I had a hard time following him. He shifted topics faster than a horse race announcer, and just when I got the gist of what he was saying, he switched back. As he went on about plans for a road trip, I loaded my coffee with sugar, nodding so he didn't think I wasn't paying attention.

He gasped. "Did you see the Grand Canyon?"

"Ah, no… I didn't stop until I got here."

He tossed the chewed straw on his napkin and took a breath. "I'm doing it again, aren't I? How about I let you talk?"

I smiled, because his scatterbrained thoughts were amusing. "I, ah… well, I'm looking for someone."

His brows popped. "And you drove all the way from Texas?"

I shrugged, because I felt foolish for having admitted it. "It's important."

"Are they missing or something?" he asked cautiously.

"Not exactly."

"Well, stranger things have happened here. Okay, Aiden from Texas. I know the area well, and I know lots of people, and they know lots of people, so who are you looking for?"

I opened my mouth, but nothing came out. How did I explain this to him? "A lost relative."

He punched his hand in the air, his face brightening exponentially, and I nearly sank into my seat as heads turned in our direction.

"Yes! You are on some kind of family history journey, aren't you? Oh, this is awesome. I love digging into the past," he exclaimed, peeling another straw.

I was at a loss for words, his jubilation rendering me speechless.

"Who are we looking for?"

49

I cleared my throat, then took a sip of coffee and said, "An elderly gentleman. I'm not sure if he still lives in the area, but he goes by the name of Bibby."

Cody pursed his lips, and I was shocked by the five-second-long silence.

"Never heard of him. Do you have an address?"

"Yeah," I said, feeling suddenly giddy at the prospect of finding this mysterious man.

As I rattled off the address, his face slowly fell.

"Damn. Just when this was getting exciting. Orange Blossom Drive doesn't exist anymore. It used to be part of an area called the Garden, but it was demolished ten years ago so they could build that hideous strip mall. I was only a kid back then, but all those old, pretty houses. I tried collecting signatures to stop it, but what can you do when the big corporations come in and buy off all your politicians? I mean, they're supposed to serve the people, not—"

I didn't hear the rest of his story. I knew I shouldn't have gotten my hopes up. Coming to Montana, I'd known the chances of Bibby still being alive were slim, and the chances that he still lived in the area were even smaller, but I'd been blindly hopeful and stupid.

"Don't worry, though," Cody said, then stuck a fresh straw in his mouth. "A majority of the garden residents still live in Valley Forge. The company that bought out the Garden was nice enough to set them up in new houses. That was the least they could do after uprooting entire families, right?"

I perked up, his words giving me hope.

"Of course, this would be a lot easier if we had his real name. I mean, Bibby has to be some sort of nick, right? Unless his parents were, like, weird. Can you imagine going through school with a name like that?"

As he droned on, I couldn't help shaking my head, amused by his process of thought.

"I'll be quiet now," Cody finally said. "But yeah. Do we have a real name to work with?"

My hand was drawn to my coat pocket where I had stashed one of the envelopes, and I was tempted to explain why I was really here, but I didn't want to come off as an impulsive fool. Remembering the question, I shook my head, apologizing for being so vague.

"Well, it wouldn't be that easy, would it? But that's part of the fun. This is like searching for buried treasure or something." He smiled, looking completely happy to be involved in my search.

I supposed he was right in a way. The letters were my map, but I wasn't sure if the search would be worth it in the end. If we managed to find Bibby, what exactly did I have to gain? A few sweet stories? Perhaps. But it hardly seemed worth the journey. *I'm here*, I mused. *Might as well give it a shot.* Besides, my guide was a gorgeous cowboy short a horse and a hat that promised to be entertaining.

"Well, if you want my advice, I think we should start at the library or city hall. The census should tell who lived at your address."

I straightened my spine, wondering why I hadn't thought of that in the beginning. Then again, I hadn't really thought this whole thing through. I said, "That sounds like a good idea."

Cody made a strangled sound. "But public access closes at two." He sat back, a slow smile spreading across his face. "I have an idea. Have breakfast with me tomorrow… say eight. Then we'll head over to city hall and see what we can dig up."

I wanted to insist we rush over there now but refrained. "Okay."

"Awesome," he said and produced a pencil. He scribbled something on his napkin.

When he handed it to me, I asked, "What's this?"

"My address. The only thing better than Mama Hen pancakes is my mother's rise-and-shine special."

My jaw fell open. "I, ah…."

"You agreed to have breakfast with me," he said, looking like a petulant five-year-old.

"Okay, I guess," I managed, feeling a little weird being invited over to someone's house who I didn't know.

"Don't worry. We're not a bunch of inbred psychos planning to chop you up and use you for fertilizer."

"That doesn't exactly inspire confidence," I sputtered, actually amused. I knew I shouldn't be, but I couldn't help it.

He winked. "In the meantime, what's on your agenda for the rest of the day?"

The hopeful look he passed me was unsettling, and I found myself loosening my jacket. I was unclear as to what he was asking, but the idea of wasting some time with him was highly appealing. I didn't drive over a thousand miles to get laid, I reminded myself. Playing it cool, I said, "Relaxation and sleep. It's been a busy few weeks."

He nodded, but I thought he looked disappointed. "Okay, Aiden. You go back to the motel and sleep, because you're going to need your energy for tomorrow."

I knew his intentions were benign, but the way he spoke got my blood pumping.

CHAPTER SEVEN

I STARED at the scribble on the napkin, then turned my attention to the two-story farmhouse down the road. I hoped I was in the right place. I didn't want to knock on someone's door this early on a Saturday only to be told I had the wrong house. I had debated all morning about whether or not I should come. People didn't just invite strangers to their house for breakfast… did they? I realized I was in a whole new world.

Figuring I'd come this far, I decided I might as well follow through. As I steered the Hummer down the path, I noticed how familiar everything looked. The fields were devoid of crops, but behind the house loomed a vast snow-covered landscape dotted with cattle. The house itself was lovely—very "cottage in the woods" with several evergreens surrounding the front yard. Christmas lights framed the porch and windows, and hideous plastic statues of Santa and his reindeer filled the small yard.

My chest got tight for a moment as I remembered what Mom's house had looked like during the holidays. She'd loved Christmas too and hadn't shied away from decking the halls, and the porch, and the barn… and whatever else she could get her hands on.

Stepping out of the car, I ran my fingers along my temples in an effort to smooth my hair. I'd spent way too long looking in the mirror, and I had to remind myself I wasn't going on a date. But these people were inviting a stranger into their home, and I wanted to appear sane despite feeling totally out of control. I marched up to the door, and the scent of cooking food hit me, eliciting an enthusiastic growl from my gut. It had been a while since I'd had a good home-cooked meal. All the fancy restaurants and catered lunches couldn't compare.

Before I could knock, the door was yanked open, the bells on the wreath clamoring, and Cody gave me the most dazzling, blinding smile I'd seen from him yet.

"Mornin', stranger," he said, looking chipper.

"Good morning."

"Come in," he said, stretching his arm out. "Oh, and don't mind the clutter. My mother is nutty for Christmas. And my father is a huge rock hound, so don't get freaked out by all the skeletons lying around."

I was utterly clueless as I stepped in, Cody moving too fast for me to keep up with. The living room was so packed with decorations and mementos, I suddenly felt claustrophobic. When I spotted a rock slab with some sort of fish fossil embedded in it, Cody's words made sense. The living room was very homey, crocheted throw blankets scattered across the couch and photographs on every wall.

A pawing at my leg caught my attention, and I looked down to find a shih tzu with a fancy haircut and dressed in a Christmas vest, smiling at me.

Cody chuckled. "This is Fabio. Isn't he fabulous?"

"He fits right in," I said good-naturedly and gave the pooch a head scratching.

"Cody, hon. Is that him?" A voice drifted to us.

"Yeah!" Cody shot back. When he looked at me, he beamed. "Come meet my mother."

Of course I'd known I'd have to meet Cody's family, but it still felt weird. Before we could get far, a tall woman dressed in a Santa Claus hat pulled me into a hug. Her grip was strong, and I awkwardly accepted it. Her perfume dug up painful memories, but the softness of her ugly Christmas sweater was lovely against my arms.

"Mom, let him breathe," Cody admonished, then explained to me, "Sorry, the holidays make her all touchy-feely."

A hand shot out, smacking him in the arm.

"Ow," Cody complained.

"Don't you start," she said, then looked at me, her baby blues dazzling. "And how long has he been hiding you from me? And oh, you are gorgeous, aren't you?"

"Mom, no!" Cody pulled her away, his cheeks colored. "Not every guy I bring home is... someone I'm involved with."

She looked at me and blinked. "Oh, well. My mistake. And what a shame, here I thought he finally got lucky."

Cody face-palmed, and I could do nothing but gape. I felt as if I were on a roller coaster, my surroundings passing by so quickly I had no idea where I was or what I was doing.

"Well, it's nice to meet you, Aiden. I'm Marge. Are you two working on a new campaign, then?" she asked.

I looked to him for direction, and he lit up, the excitement in his eyes dancing. "No, Aiden is on a quest! He came all the way from Texas in search of long-lost family."

"Oh!" she gasped. Taking me by the arm, she led me to the couch. "Did Cody tell you about the Bannar lineage?"

I shook my head, dumbfounded. I was still stuck on the idea that this charming, gorgeous guy was gay and possibly available. I plopped my butt on the sofa, reminding myself I wasn't here to get laid.

"We're a bunch of criminals!" Cody chimed in.

"Hush!" his mother hissed and waved him away. "This is my story. But he's right, you know. At least my great-great-grandfather was an outlaw."

As she went on with her family's story, Cody shoved a tall glass of OJ in front of me, and I took a sip, nodding in an attempt to keep up. Cody was prone to interrupt with hilarious comments, his enthusiasm soaking into me. I couldn't help the laugh as she wound up the dish towel that had been over her shoulder and whipped him in the behind.

"You're not too old for a spanking," she chided good-naturedly.

Cody cackled. "Mom, not in front of guests."

"Anyway." She smiled at me. "Cattle theft might not sound like a big deal, but back then it was very serious, and he made a lot of money, but the law eventually caught up with him."

"And in order to escape prosecution, Great-Great-Granddaddy changed his last name and moved north to Montana," Cody said. "And here we are."

"Boy, you are stealing my show."

"Sorry," he said meekly.

"What's wit' the arguin'?" An elderly man tsked as he came in.

"Hey, Unc." Cody beamed, hugging the man and patting him on the back. He frowned, then leaned in. "Have you been smoking again?"

The guy craned his head back. "No."

"Uh-huh." Cody sighed. "You should know better."

"I ain't but had one drag."

"Now isn't the time," Marge interjected. "We have a guest."

Cody's uncle turned to regard me, his aged eyes shrewd. "Does he like to hunt? I tol' you not to bring a man home unless he likes to hunt, di'n't I?"

Cody growled. "No, he's not my—this is Aiden. He's from Texas and looking for a lost relative. I've offered my services in finding the guy... or girl. I'm not really sure."

When Cody turned to me, I said hoarsely, "No, it's definitely a man we're looking for."

"Maybe you can help us, Uncle Roger? Do you know anyone named Bibby that lived in the Garden?"

"Bibby? Is that some kind of hippie name?" The man scowled. "No, I don' think I do."

A commotion went up as two older ladies barreled in, hugging Marge, then pulling Cody into their group hug. When it quieted, I realized they were looking at me, their twin expressions intrigued. I suddenly felt hot, as if I were the focus of attention. Still, I could feel the warmth of Cody's family, and I was amazed at the easiness between them.

"Aunties, this is Aiden—"

"Oh, it's nice to meet you!" they said in unison, and I stood to accept their hugs, completely overwhelmed by the warm reception. I had expected cool regard, not this. These people didn't even know me and they seemed intent on treating me like a good friend.

"Wow! Cody's finally scored, hasn't he?" one said to the other as she ran her eyes up and down my body.

The other nodded, and Cody face-palmed again.

"Give him room," Marge said. "Breakfast is almost ready. Cody, have you seen your brother?"

"He's probably out in the barn looking at porn mags," Cody said.

Marge punched him in the arm.

"What? Wasn't he there the last two times you went looking for him?"

"Lord, why didn't you bless me with more daughters?" She sighed and disappeared into the kitchen.

Cody grinned at me. "Sorry, my family is a little weird. I guess I should have warned you."

I shook my head, intending to say something, but the words were lost. Truthfully, I was enjoying the banter and light-hearted teasing. It made me feel like I was in a *home*. I tried to remember when my family had felt like this, but I couldn't really recall such a time. When my parents had been married, dinners had always revolved around cold, clinical conversation concerning business matters and school grades, and Missy would dominate the table, detailing how she'd triumphed over one thing or another.

"Aiden?" Cody prompted, a stubby pencil stuck in the corner of his mouth. "Did we freak you out?"

"No. I just didn't expect such a warm welcome," I admitted.

"Well, like I said. We're a friendly bunch. Most of us anyway. There are a few people you might want to stay clear of... the Republican types. Crap, please tell me you're not Republican. I don't want to keep insulting you over and over."

"I'm not really anything."

A man entered through the front door, and Cody jumped to his feet. "Dad, come meet Aiden. The guy I told you would be joining us for breakfast? And no… we're not a thing. I'm just helping him."

I wondered if Cody made a habit of bringing a lot of men home.

The guy motioned to his lips, and Cody gasped, sticking the pencil in his pocket.

"How long have you been nibblin'? You're going to ruin your teeth—"

"Not now, please," Cody whispered harshly. "We have a guest."

"Right," the man said and turned to me, his expression blank.

I got up to meet him, accepting his hand.

"Nice, firm handshake. That's good. I'm Dwayne. Welcome to our humble home."

"Thanks?" I muttered.

Dwayne turned to Cody. "Where's your brother?"

"Where do you think?" Cody snickered.

The man sighed and headed out the door, whispering curses. "When I was your age I never…."

"You have a lot of siblings?" I asked before I could help myself.

"Oh yeah. Let's see. There's Jake and Jesse, who are in the military. Then there's Clarice, who just got married and is on her honeymoon in Vegas. I need to add gambling to my bucket list, but I figure the money could be spent better places, you know? My other sister, Betty, is in college… she'll be the first doctor of the family. Who else? Oh, Adam, who is at work. He manages the local grocery, so he usually leaves early. And then there's my youngest brother, Elroi, who likes to hide in the barn."

"Yeah… I was like that once."

Cody looked at me askance. "He's twenty-two."

"Oh," I said and blushed, feeling silly.

"Food's ready!" Marge called from the kitchen.

Cody beamed. "Come on, let's get us some chow."

I followed him into the kitchen, where several people were standing around and chatting noisily. The smell of food hit me, and I inhaled deeply. Marge spotted me and handed me a plate. The classic Southern breakfast of biscuits and gravy, fluffy pancakes, sausage, and bacon had been set out buffet style. I was eager to dig in.

I set two slices of bacon on my plate.

Cody smacked his lips and proceeded to load my plate.

"Don't be modest. Seriously, Mom will take it as insult if you don't loosen your pants."

I had to wonder what it was with moms that insisted on feeding their kids until bursting, but the thought was nice, if not a little uncomfortable. I smiled good-naturedly as he piled my plate high, talking about how the pork sausage was an old family recipe that his great-aunt had buried in the yard because she wanted to keep it secret. Marge had only discovered it after redoing the garden bed. I tried to keep up, but Cody flew through the story so fast my brain didn't have time to absorb the words.

"Okay, I think that is everything. Let's sit on the patio where it's quieter."

As he led me to the back of the house, I was relieved to find that the patio was enclosed and heated. As we settled in on wicker chairs, Cody cursed.

"Forgot the salt. Be right back."

Before I could acknowledge him, he was gone, and I realized I'd left my OJ inside. Tentatively, I set my plate on a matching table and slid back into the house. I retrieved my glass, nodding to a little old lady who blinked at me from behind big glasses.

"Tell Timmy I said he's late. Will ya do that for me, Frankie?"

"Sure…." I quickly retreated to the patio, only to stop dead in my tracks. My plate was on the floor, the mound of food gone, and Fabio was wheezing. I gaped. I'd only been gone for a minute.

"Fabio!" Cody gasped and picked him up, then hit his chest. The dog choked once, then licked his snout and looked at me as if I had more. "I told you, you need to chew your food. Don't scare me like that."

As Fabio scampered back into the house, Cody said, "Sorry, I should have told you. He will steal food in an instant. He was rescued from a hoarder and was so emaciated when they found him. He's still in that mentality where he has to eat everything as quickly as possible. I wish I could volunteer at the shelter more often, but I'm a busy boy these days. From the moment I saw him, I knew I was his. Our old bloodhound had just passed, so…. Yeah, I'll get you another plate. Then, when you're done eating, we'll hit the library. Sound good?"

"Okay," I said and smiled, amused. With Cody's enthusiasm, I knew my time here would be anything but boring.

"AND THIS is the florist, but you don't need to know that, do you?" Cody said as he showed me around town.

We had spent the last hour driving in circles, Cody pointing out all the good places to eat and the top entertainment hotspots along with facilities that had no use to me, like florists. Still, it was hard not to be charmed by the guy. I learned the town was famous for biscuits and gravy and some old bridge, Cody going on and on about how he liked to sit on the edge and listen to the water flow.

"Here!" he exclaimed.

He pulled into the parking lot of the Valley Forge Library, and excitement got into my system, my insides bouncing a little. I might get to meet Bibby tonight. What would I say? I hadn't thought past finding the guy.

"Okay, let's go," Cody said, his tone laced with enthusiasm.

I followed him into the library, and he stopped at the desk to talk with the librarian for a long while, discussing mundane things in detail. I rocked on my feet, my eyes drawn over to the computers. Thankfully, she got distracted with work and Cody led me to an available desk. We sat down, our knees touching, his body heat soaking into me. Just what I needed…. Being attracted to this guy wasn't going to help.

Cody focused on the computer, flipping through the years of newspaper articles and commenting about the sad demise of the Garden. When he pulled up some photos, I could see why he was so disheartened. Dozens of old, beautiful houses had been demolished, decades of history wiped away for a strip mall.

"I remember going to the Garden with my sister to help her sell Girl Scout cookies. I can't recall the lady's name, but she was so sweet. She told us she was diabetic and couldn't eat them but gave my sister five dollars to put toward her trip to the Grand Canyon. I came back the next day and mowed her lawn. Of course she forced me to accept another five bucks. Now her house is gone. I'm pretty sure she passed away too. Back then she was ancient. Damn, Aiden... all that history and memories cleared away by bulldozers for a frickin' strip mall. It makes me want to cry."

I tried to relate to Cody's sadness. I supposed I would be devastated if Mom's farmhouse was demolished, but the little old lady of his story was nothing more than an acquaintance. It was clear from the tone of his voice, Cody was the type of person who had bawled openly when Old Yeller had been shot.

"Anyway," he said, shrugging. "I guess it's natural for the world to change."

As we scrolled through old stories concerning the Garden, Cody went on talking about the good ole days when being a kid was easy. I wholeheartedly agreed and let him know, his little smile making me all fuzzy inside. Eventually he came to the end, and by the time the library was getting ready to close for the day, we were back where we started.

"Well, that was a bust," Cody said, shutting down the computer. "I'm sorry, Aiden. I was hopin' we'd find something here. Next step county records, but it's really late and I got to get some work in today."

I looked at my cell phone, and my jaw nearly detached from my skull. I couldn't believe it was almost four in the afternoon. The hours had just slipped by without me noticing. Then again, when you're having fun... and being around Cody was entertaining, to say the least. Realizing I'd kept him for so long, I started apologizing.

"I'm so sorry. I should have known you would have obligations."

"Nah, don't worry about it. I don't really have to be anywhere. I try to work at least four hours a day, but sometimes I do get distracted," he said, ruffling his hair. "I'm a blogger, mostly video, and I've made a promise to my followers to do at least three vids a week. It takes time… recording, uploading, and editing. It's really work. So no slacking."

My brows rose. "I didn't realize blogging could be considered a job."

"Oh yeah!"

He beamed, and I realized I'd hit that special spot that would have him chatting endlessly.

"I have a lot of followers, so the commission I make from ads is pretty decent. But more than that, it's the job. I love connecting with people. I do all sorts of stuff… politics, entertainment, social events—" He looked at me askance. "Question and answers about yours truly. It's a lot of fun."

As we left the library, Cody went on about how he'd gotten into blogging back in high school, when he'd started his school's first Gay and Straight Student Alliance and was on the school's newspaper staff. He didn't stop talking until we were in front of my motel room.

Taking a deep breath, Cody said, "So, yeah. That's how I got into it."

I nodded. "Well, it's great to enjoy what you do."

"And what's your occupation? Gigi said you're some kind of businessman?"

"Ah… yeah. I did the whole business-school thing. My father owns several stores down in Texas, so it was obvious I— Well, it's not really all that enjoyable, but it pays the bills."

When he looked at me expectantly, I fidgeted, hesitant to tell him what I really did. I imagined he wouldn't approve. Heck, I didn't approve.

"Oh, right!" he said louder than necessary. "You probably want to relax. Sorry, I can be…. Tell you what. You take it easy for the evening, and I'll drop by tomorrow morning and pick you up. Then we'll head over to city hall. I'm sure we'll find something there."

"Sounds good," I said, trying to hide my enthusiasm. I was seriously looking forward to hanging out with Cody some more. He was a breath of fresh air that I realized I needed.

"Awesome!" He winked. "Well, don't hesitate to call me if you need anything."

"Okay."

With that, we parted, and when I was in my room, I went straight to my laptop and googled Cody's blog. It was mostly situated on YouTube, and I started going through his videos. I learned very quickly that he was an extremely passionate, caring person, from his political views to his charity efforts. I envied the man who would eventually steal his heart. The hours slipped away as I went back months, his Q&As hilarious. Cody was also a very honest person, sharing some of his high school struggles with being openly gay, but what grabbed my attention was his sex advice.

Oh God, I seriously needed to get laid. Here I was at ten o'clock at night, trolling Cody's blog for naughty snippets, and he wasn't shy about it. I actually blushed as I watched him detail tips for bottoming. Closing my laptop, I took several deep breaths, only to realize I was hard. I told myself I was going straight to bed and get a good night's rest, but that plan was quickly squashed as I got comfortable.

Okay, so how was it possible to not be attracted to the man? Not only was he gorgeous, but he had the personality to back it up. His farm-boy looks were just the wrapping, and what was inside was even better.

I gave in and got naked, the sheets nice against my bare skin. I relaxed and grabbed my cock, summoning an image of Cody in front of the camera, talking about how to give the best blowjob ever. His eyes had been dark, as if he were aroused, but his tone was light, as if he were talking about the weather. The guy was born for the camera.

It wasn't long before the orgasm gathered, the explosion stronger than I expected. As I came, I focused on Cody and his dazzling smile, the release doing a hell of a lot to mellow me out. Exhausted, I collapsed, grinning like a fool. Though I knew anything between us wasn't an option, I could expect I'd enjoy being in his company if only because Cody was a bright fucking light in my dark little world, and I could use some illumination.

CHAPTER EIGHT

FOR THE second time in two days, I found myself staring at the little farmhouse surrounded by decorated evergreens. Cody had called in the morning to let me know he had exciting news. It took me a few minutes to get it out of him as he droned on about distant family relations, but it appeared that one of his aunts had lived in the Garden for a brief time and she was coming over for dinner. So I had been invited to have supper with the Bannars. I had wanted to insist we go through the county records, but I knew it would probably be fruitless. I couldn't complain about having to spend more time with him, though. I realized I was looking for an excuse to not go back to Texas because the sooner I found Bibby, the sooner I'd have to return and face my father.

Cutting the engine, I took a deep breath, then stepped out of the Hummer. I smoothed my jacket as I climbed the porch stairs. Cody was at the door in an instant, looking spectacular in a button-down denim shirt and jeans, his smile radiant. Heat raced to my cheeks as I recalled what I'd done last night.

"Aiden?" Cody prompted.

"Sorry."

"I agree the weather is nice, but— Oh! They are talking snow next week. Do you get a lot of snow in Texas?"

"Not too much," I said, seeing him lying in a stack of hay… naked. Shit, I was in trouble.

"That sucks, seriously. I love snow! It makes everything pretty, you know? But snowball fights and skiing, and cold winter nights with hot chocolate…. Are you going to come in?"

"Yeah," I mumbled as I stepped in.

Fabio welcomed me happily, pawing at my legs and begging to be picked up. A Christmas sweater covered his body, and he had miniature blue bows on his ears. The little guy was adorable, and I gave him a thorough head scratching. Before I knew what hit me, Marge pulled me into a big hug, welcoming me again, and I felt as if I'd been here a dozen times despite everyone being strangers.

"Come on. I'll introduce you to Aunt Edna," Cody said.

I followed him, the stairs creaking as we climbed to the second level. I ran my eyes over all the pictures hanging on the walls, snapshots of Cody's big family, some yellowed from age. It was nice to see such mementos. Mom had kept several photos around the house, and I could see the warmth in these people's faces. This was a real family. A reflection of what Mom and I had shared.

"That's me," Cody said, pointing to a picture of a little boy.

I leaned in, a smile arching over my lips. He must have been five or six, and he was dressed as a pirate for Halloween, his face split by a smile as he held up a hooked hand. "You look like you were a handful."

He glanced at me for a moment, then sputtered a laugh. "You have no idea. Mom made the costume for me... after I decided I didn't want to be a devil. We donated the demon costume she had made, but she didn't seem to mind having to make a whole other costume. I was such a rug rat."

"I always thought rats were cute," I said before I could stop myself.

Laughing, Cody led me down the hall and turned into a bedroom. I was glad he couldn't see my blush. The senile old lady I had met the day before was sitting in a chair, fiddling with yarn.

Cody gave her a big hug.

"Have you seen Timmy?" she inquired.

"Oh yeah, he told me to tell you he's going to be late again," Cody said good-naturedly.

"I knew it. He's always late!"

"Goodness, boy." A woman obviously related to Marge came in behind me, the resemblance uncanny. "You've gotten big."

Cody turned to regard her, patting his chest. "I work out."

The woman winked at me and gestured with her hands. "I remember him when he was this big. It seems every time I visit, Cody is bigger and bigger."

"Edna, this is Aiden. I'm helping him find someone. Aiden, this is my aunt Edna."

She tugged me into a suffocating hug, but I was quickly growing used to it. When she held me at arm's length, she asked Cody, "Is this about the Bibby person you were going on about earlier?"

"Yes! Bibby lived in the Garden...." Cody blinked at me. "I don't really know anything else."

I apologized, realizing I'd been rather vague. "I don't know that much about him, but I'm sure Bibby is just a pet name. He would be old now, in his eighties or nineties. He, ah... lived in the Garden back in the late fifties."

"Goodness! Well, that's before my time. I was one of the residents who was bought out—"

"Yeah, and she'd just purchased the house a few years earlier. Still had a mortgage on it, but did they care about that? Nope. Greedy SOBs," Cody interjected. "Sorry, Auntie."

"Well, they were nice enough to pay off what I owed, plus I received a nice little incentive. I guess I can't complain." She shrugged, shaking her head. "But for your mystery person... at the time there were several elderly folk I knew but none going by the name Bibby. Do you have an address?"

As Cody and Edna looked at me expectantly, I bit my lip in indecision. I was still reluctant to tell Cody why I was really here and just who Bibby was, but I figured being so vague was hindering our investigation. I gave them the address.

"Oh dear. I'm afraid Orange Blossom Drive was on the other side from where I lived."

"The Garden wasn't very big, only a few blocks, but wasn't Orange Blossom Drive a horseshoe?" Cody asked.

"That's right," Edna said. "I'm trying to think if I knew any older people there. If I recall, about four or five houses sat on the drive."

As they went back and forth about the logistics, and Cody talked about someone's bizarre lawn ornaments, I realized I wasn't as crushed as I should be. I didn't know if it was spending time with this man or getting a big dose of freedom, but I didn't feel fazed at all. Eventually Cody ran out of steam, and Edna wished me luck in my search before leaving the room.

"I'm sorry, Aiden. Damn, I hoped she might have known the guy."

I shrugged. "It's okay."

"No, I mean… we should have gone to city hall today, but I really thought Edna would pan out. But don't fret! I have a plan."

I cocked a brow.

Before Cody could speak, Marge called from down the stairs that dinner was ready.

"Hold that thought," Cody said, then turned to his grandmother. "Come on, Grams. Din-din is waiting."

"I won't eat until Timmy gets home."

"I think Timmy is downstairs."

"Oh, is Timmy home? He's always late, you know?"

"Yep."

When we were downstairs, a commotion filled the house, several conversations buzzing. I nodded to Cody's father, who was relaxing in an old rocking chair, then accepted hugs from the twins. When I entered the kitchen, I spotted several people I hadn't met yet, but Cody was right on it. He introduced his siblings, and I accepted handshake after handshake.

"And this is Elroi, who has decided to come out of his hidey-hole for a bit," Cody said.

"It's getting cold out," the man refuted.

I did a double take but accepted his hand, his dark skin contrasting with mine. He flipped his baseball cap to the front and gave me a toothy but friendly smile. "Welcome, bro."

"Thanks," I muttered.

Cody leaned in and whispered, "We're adopted. In case you were wondering."

"Oh." I hadn't expected it, but it explained the mishmash of Cody's siblings. I wanted to ask more about it but didn't want to come off rude. It was curious to me that this family of unrelated people could be so warm with each other when my own flesh and blood was disgusted by me.

"Don't be shy, Aiden," Marge said, handing me a plate. "Help yourself. But do save a little room for dessert."

"Yes, ma'am."

As with breakfast, dinner had been set out buffet style, and I was a lot less reserved as I loaded my plate with pork chops and mashed potatoes. Cody nodded, and I followed him out to the patio, where we took our seats, the commotion cut to a steady hum.

We ate in silence—mostly, Cody having to take time out of an endless stream of information to eat—but the environment was relaxed, the sound of his family enjoying themselves and the distant moos of the cattle loosening my body. As I filled my stomach with home-cooked goodness, I did my best to keep my eyes on anything but the man sitting across from me. But my attention was constantly drawn to him. I wasn't sure why I was so attracted to him.

"Does it weird you out that we're all adopted?" Cody asked out of the blue.

The question was so unexpected, I didn't know how to answer. "Why would it?"

He shrugged, but I could see from his expression that he thought it had.

"Stereotypes about us street kids, I guess."

"No, I just didn't expect it. It's nice to see, though," I said cordially. "If anything, I'm the odd one out here."

He laughed, and I found myself smiling. He tipped his head at my plate. "Can I get you round two?"

"No. Your mom said save room for dessert."

He took my plate. "Be right back."

"Okay."

When he was gone, I sighed and closed my eyes. Now that I'd eaten, I felt better. And interacting with so many friendly folks did something to bolster my hopes concerning my own family. I realized that my coming out had been something of a shock, and things could be said in the heat of the moment that were later regretted. I resolved to give my father a little time with the news before phoning him.

The creak of the door woke me up.

Cody smiled as he took his seat. "Did you fall asleep?"

"Halfway there. It's been a while since I had a good home-cooked meal and such... peace. I don't get it as much as I'd like."

"Let me guess.... Houston?"

I hesitated, wanting to keep a distance between us. "No... I grew up around the farm scene."

"Really?" he exclaimed and sat forward, his interest sky-high.

"Yeah. Corn feed mostly, but that was a long time ago. I grew up, went to college, and got a degree. I haven't been on a farm in years, and I didn't realize how much I missed it."

"That's awesome. We have something in common, then." His cheeks reddened, and he fidgeted. "I was four when Mom and Dad brought me home. Dad introduced me to the life, and the first time I tried helping him... well, it didn't turn out so well. By the time the day's chores were done, I looked like something from *Swamp Thing*."

I tried to hide my laugh but failed.

"It's okay. You can laugh. It's just one of my many misadventures of life on the farm. I love it, though. Anyway, before I get sidetracked, I thought we might do this."

I looked at the piece of paper he held up and frowned. It was a questionnaire to request information about family ancestry.

"It says it can take up to eight weeks to hear back, but I figured it wouldn't hurt to at least inquire."

"You know, that's not a bad idea."

Cody beamed, his eyes crinkling in the corners. He pulled out a pen from behind his ear. He asked me questions, and I answered, watching as he filled the questionnaire in. They were the basics—family surname, logistics, etc. I wasn't entirely truthful, considering

Bibby wasn't related, but I played along. I knew in eight weeks' time, I'd be back in Texas at the very least.

Cody stuck the pen in the corner of his mouth and said, "Okay, I think that is it. All we have to do is mail it in."

"Isn't there a fee?"

His eyes shot to me, and he cleared his throat. "Kinda. But no worries. I got it."

"Are you kidding? No way," I said.

His lips pulled up. "It's the least I can do. I said I'd help you, remember?"

"Yes, but that is different."

"How so?" he asked, blinking at me as if he was really clueless.

Damn this guy. I didn't understand him at all, but the gesture was sweet, and—

Cody sputtered and choked, a stream of blue ink cascading down his chin. Agape, I could do nothing but watch as he excused himself and rushed into the house. Not a moment later a commotion went up, Marge's voice ringing clear.

"I told you, boy, no pens in this house!"

"Sorry, Mom. Adam must have brought it home from work—"

The shouting eventually died down, and I sat there, wondering what had happened. I waited for Cody to return, but the minutes stretched by, and I debated walking in. But what would I say? Truthfully, I was a little embarrassed for him.

The door creaked and Marge came out, smiling ruefully.

"How was dinner?" she asked.

I perked up. "Very good, thank you so much."

"Good. Listen, Cody is embarrassed about what happened. I told him it's not a big deal, but he asked me to tell you—"

"Okay. Thanks. Will you let him know the *Smurfs* was my favorite cartoon?"

A slow smile split her face, and she pointed at me. "Don't you move."

"Yes, ma'am."

She retreated into the house, only to emerge a minute later with Cody being dragged by his shirt.

"Please, don't…," he begged.

Marge pushed him out the door. "Aiden, you want to tell him what you told me?"

My brows popped up. "That the *Smurfs* was my favorite cartoon?"

Cody's attention shot to me, his face brightening, his blue lips curling up. Marge made a sound of satisfaction, then left us. Reluctantly, Cody dragged his feet to the chair and sat down.

He took a deep breath, then slowly let it out. "I have pica, and that happens sometimes. We're not supposed to have pens in the house for that very reason, but Adam brought one home, and I didn't think completing the questionnaire with a pencil would be appropriate."

"Oh." It was all I could say.

He looked at me, his eyes wide. "You don't know what that is, do you? It's hard to explain. It's like OCD, where I chew and eat things…. Sorry. I'm weirding you out, aren't I?"

"No. I didn't know something like that existed."

"Oh, yeah. It's just one of my many quirks. It was hard at first. I had a bad habit of eating crayons and getting sick. But I learned how to handle it in high school, and now it's not so bad. It sometimes acts up, especially when I get nervous—"

He stopped, and I wanted to ask why he was nervous, but I refrained, figuring getting him riled up wouldn't be good. I silently beamed, wondering if I had anything to do with it.

"I mean, it can be so bad for some people that they eat soap and rocks…." He ran his fingers through his hair. "You like the *Smurfs*, huh?"

I laughed, and it felt good. "Smurfette is my girl."

Cody nearly jumped out of his chair. "Oh, I know!"

As he went on and on, detailing the show's entire run in a long breath, my cheeks started to hurt, and I realized I was smiling.

"I haven't seen the movie yet. Would you like to take a walk? It's going to be a little while before dessert, and I need to burn as many calories as I can. I mean, I'm surprised I've managed to keep my figure with my mom's cooking."

"You know, that sounds nice."

WE WALKED along the fence, Cody telling me about raising cattle. As I listened, I pulled in cool air, my lungs stretching wonderfully. When he paused to take a breath, I asked, "Milk cows or beef?"

"Beef. When I was a kid, I thought it was sad having to kill them and went vegan for a month. I had a lot of strange ideas when I was young. I'm still very opposed to the mass-market beef trade… not just inhumane treatment of their animals, but all the antibiotics they inject. Sorry, I should warn you not to ask me anything. Once I get started, it's hard to stop. But issues like these are important."

I grinned. "It's nice to have someone to talk to."

"You mean talked to?" he teased, bumping my elbow with his own.

I nodded, and we headed toward the line of evergreens, the mountains looming in the darkening sky. The crisp scent of pine was heavy but welcome, the nippy air refreshing. "It's really gorgeous out here."

"Isn't it, though? I've been to a lot of places, but I don't think I could ever leave Montana permanently. This is my home… with Mom and Dad and my sisters and brothers and my friends. And the cattle and horses and the mountains. Although I will see every state at least once. When that is done, I'd like to take a trip to Africa and Australia… oh, and Scotland. Enough about me, tell me about you."

I opened my mouth, but nothing came out. I laughed and shook my head. "Easier said than done."

"I get it. Mysterious stranger from a mysterious place with mysterious intentions. Don't you think I've realized you got secrets?" He grinned. "Teasing of course."

73

I sighed, glad he wasn't willing to press the point. "Can I ask you something?"

"Yep. I'm a pretty open person. I mean, most of my family watches my videos and… ah, I have some questionable subject matter on there."

I kept it to myself that I was aware of what he was referring to.

"Aiden?" he prompted.

The question was poised on the edge of my lips, but I shook my head. "Never mind."

"No, tell me. I'm really nosey, and it's going to bother me for a very long time if you don't tell me."

I cocked a brow at him. "Guilt trip?"

"No way. Blackmail."

A laugh bubbled up.

"Seriously. I know I'm a motor mouth, but I have big ears too."

After a moment I managed, "I was curious about… high school and coming out."

He stopped and pegged me with an intense look. I could feel his eyes on me like hands rummaging through a chest, and I knew speculations were flying through his head.

"Wait… did you see my blog?"

Now it was my turn to fidget. "I googled it."

"How far did you go back?"

"Not too far," I lied.

Clearing his throat, he shrugged. "Well… that's good. The more people, the better. Thanks for the pennies, by the way. But to answer your question, it wasn't so bad. Most of my friends supported me, but there were a few who were opposed to it."

"No, that's not what I meant," I stumbled. When he looked at me in expectancy, I said, "How did your family handle it?"

I could see on his face he had a whole slew of questions lined up for me, but to my surprise he held them back. "I was terrified of telling them."

We started walking again, and for the first time since being in his presence, it was quiet, the silence feeling out of place. I assumed he was troubled by the question, and I opened my mouth to apologize, but he cut me off.

"It took me years to get it in my head that these people who had taken me home truly loved me despite all my problems with the pica and ADD, not to mention the damned dentist bills. I thought I was a burden and that being gay would just add another layer to my rotten onion, so it took me a long time to find the courage to tell them. I thought if they knew, they'd send me back. Ten years ago, it wasn't very accepted in the community, but... yeah. It was a huge relief when I finally told Mom. Do you want to know what she said?"

I nodded because my throat was suddenly dry.

"She said, 'Perfect! Then you can help your sister choose her prom dress, because the girl is giving me a headache.'"

We shared an amused smile, but I was dubious. "Really? That easy?"

"I was completely shell-shocked. I had prepared myself for a lecture and compiled a list of answers to certain questions, but she just shrugged and hugged me and told me it didn't change the way she felt and that I was her son. Damn it!"

"What?" I gasped as he punched me in the arm.

"You're going to make me cry."

Grinning, I rubbed the sore spot. When we came to the forest's edge, Cody leaned against a tree. "Is that all you wanted to know?"

"Yes."

"You sure about that?" he asked, his brow rising.

I knew I had given myself away by asking such a personal and specific question, but I didn't regret it. It was still a mystery to me that his family had so readily accepted him. "There was no one that—"

"Had a hard time accepting it?" Cody finished. "Dad was honest with me. He told me he didn't understand it, but it didn't make him love me any less. My uncle was adamant that I judge the worth of any boyfriends on whether or not they liked to hunt. No... my family was pretty good about it. Just my—"

Cody looked away, his eyes dimming, and I thought I'd hit a nerve. I realized we knew so little about each other and it was inappropriate of me to ask such a personal question.

When his eyes settled back on me, I knew what was coming.

"Is there another reason you came all the way up here besides looking for someone you never met? I mean, you don't even know their name. Most people don't… I'm sorry. I'll zip my lips."

He made a motion indicating a zipper, coaxing a smile from me. I wanted to tell him the truth, his hopeful expression pulling me in, urging me gently to confide in him. I knew if I did he'd handle me with care, but I didn't want this happy, amazing guy to know how screwed up I was. That and I had managed to put my mother's death on the back burner, and I was afraid mentioning it would uncover the pain.

I wanted to be like him… to have a family like the Bannars, and the fact that I didn't, hurt. Before I realized what I was doing, I took several steps in his direction, just wanting to be near the warmth Cody radiated. I hadn't intended to get as close as I had, our jackets brushing. His eyes widened, the blue of his irises luminous, his parted, ink-stained lips moist. In the second that I ran my eyes over his face, I noticed so many things about him—like the light spatter of freckles across his cheeks and the tiny scar marring his eyebrow. This close, he smelled like lumber and soap.

I was unable to stop the roll, and fuck, I didn't want to. I pressed my lips to his and swallowed his gasp, his scent intoxicating. He hardly responded, and my senses returned. I backed away, feeling very silly.

"I'm sorry. That was—"

My words were cut off as he gripped my jacket and pulled me in. We crashed, and I moaned into his mouth as he kissed me senseless, his tongue commanding mine.

Cody broke away. "Oh God. Do I taste like ink?"

Feeling like a million bucks, I pulled him back to me and took my time, savoring the warm wetness of his tongue and his hot breath. The wind was chill around us, but his body heat sunk into me, shielding me from the frigid air.

"I have a mint," he said between breaths.

I backed him up against the tree, and his hands dropped down to my ass, his fingers digging into my back pockets. He felt so good against me that I thought I would come right then and there. It wasn't just the physical feeling of being close to another man, but the release of stress did me a hell of a lot of good. I needed the emotional connection as much as the physical pleasure, and I was certain Cody was the cuddling type.

"You want to go somewhere quieter?" he inquired, his voice shaky.

I regarded him for a moment. I told myself not to get involved and not start something with this amazing guy, but I couldn't help myself. I nodded, and he grinned, his cheeks mottled. We walked side by side through the woods, trading shy smiles. I wanted to ask where he was taking me, but I didn't want to break the peace. The sound of rushing water grew louder as we walked, until a beaten road cut through the forest. An old covered bridge stretched across a stream in the process of freezing over, and I took a moment to admire it.

"Was this the bridge you were talking about?" I inquired as we walked onto it, the boards creaking under my weight.

"Yep. Over a hundred years old and the last covered bridge remaining in the county. The road isn't used anymore, but the bridge is a landmark, so it's going to be around for a long time. It's kinda in the middle of nowhere, so no big companies wanting to bulldoze on through."

When his heated glance dropped to my lips, I teased, "Is there a reason you brought me to such a remote place?"

A sly smirk arched over his lips, and he surrounded me, my back bumping against a wooden beam. He leaned in, languorously closing the distance. He took my lips slow, the kiss gentle, and I followed his lead. I responded to every sweep and lick. Cody was an amazing kisser, and now that the surprise had passed, he took the lead.

His hand dropped to my hip, and I groaned, his erection pressing into mine. My heart drumming in my ears, he kissed my jaw, his words a hot whisper.

"No one really comes around here."

"Yeah?" I croaked. I skimmed my fingers across the button of his jeans. When hot, smooth skin met my hand, I hissed. I wanted to rip his clothes from his body and hold him close.

"A little more?" he inquired, taking my lobe between his teeth.

I bit my lip to keep from groaning and nodded. The moment his hand found my erection, I wanted to cry out in victory. I needed a warm body pressed against me, hot breath across my neck. I needed the release Cody promised with nothing but the water and trees to play witness. I didn't want to have to worry about my father walking in on me or what my orientation might make Mom think about her son. I just wanted to forget my life and exist in this moment—it was simpler that way.

Relaxing against the beam, I closed my eyes as Cody tugged on my jeans, popping the button. The sound of my zipper was beautiful, and when his cool palm dipped in to cup me, I yelped.

"Sorry!" he said, grinning. "Cold hands. I need something to warm them on."

I chuckled. "Please, let me help you with that."

The amusement was blown away by lust as he worked me slowly, his thumb teasing the glans. I knew it wasn't going to take long, so I busied my hands, freeing his cock.

"Oh God, it's cold," he whispered, jutting his hips into mine.

I was a passenger on the ride, my motions reflecting his as he positioned our dicks against one another and rocked against me. Digging my fingers into his jacket, I hung on, the passion and excitement of frotting in the woods sending my mind reeling. It was overwhelming and highly welcome.

His lips came against my neck, and I stabbed my fingers through his hair, holding him close. On some level, the whole thing felt like a dream… a desperate fantasy. It wasn't long before we were both panting and groaning, the orgasm rising quickly. Cody came first, a rush of wet heat rocketing me off the world. I joined him, the noise of the water below unable to cover my growl.

"Christ," he whispered, clutching on to me.

Grinning, I didn't let him go for a long while, the solidness of his body comforting.

CHAPTER NINE

"WELL, I guess I shouldn't be bummed, considering we didn't have much of a chance anyway," I said as we left city hall the next day.

"We do have some names, though. It's a place to start," Cody said, his infectious smile ushering my little storm cloud away.

We'd spent most of the afternoon in the archive, and while there was no mention of a Bibby, we had compiled a list of some of the people who had lived at the address over the years the letters had been written. Of course, Cody had been a ray of sunshine, his countless stories captivating, and I found myself constantly drawn to him. The way his face lit up was spectacular, and his propensity to shift subjects so quickly was like a roller coaster ride I was surprised to find I enjoyed.

He patted his stomach. "You hungry? I am."

The look he gave me made me think he had something else in mind, and I grinned. Yesterday had been amazing and so unexpected that I was still unsure if it had really happened. When he'd shown up at the motel in the morning bright-eyed and bushy-haired, he'd made no mention of the time we had shared on the bridge, and I was wondering if he might like to do it again. I didn't want to shatter the easiness between us, so I pushed that thought to the back of my mind.

"I know a good place. It's a bit of a drive, but it's entirely worth it. And this dude I know… I think he is related to one of the names on the list."

Cody's version of a "bit of a drive" ended up being forty-five minutes into another town. We quickly left the quaint peace of Valley Forge and cut through the woods, several factories looming against the mountains. He gave me some background about rallying the townsfolk into pressuring the county board to impose sanctions and succeeding. As he went on, his voice rose and his cheeks plumped in jubilation, his passion coming through. I wondered what it felt like to be so passionate about something.

"We weren't trying to get them shut down. I mean, the county needs the jobs, but it could be done cleaner. Anyway, we're almost there."

The diner came out of nowhere as Cody made a hard right onto a dirt road. The place was surrounded by pines, and it reminded me of a cottage in the middle of a vast forest. It was packed, and Cody parked in the back, informing me that he knew the owner well.

"Who do you think this guy is related to on the list?"

He tapped his fingers on the paper. "My friend's name is Albie Smith."

"As is Thomas Smith?" I asked, agape. "That's a common surname."

A flush colored his cheeks. "Yeah I know, but I'm hungry, and I figured what can it hurt? But treasure hunts are like that, you know? You gotta look at every possibility. Everything is a potential clue."

As he droned on, I shook my head, completely amused. I supposed he was right about this whole thing being a treasure hunt, and I wanted to tell him the truth of what we were looking for and why. I was sure he could understand my brash decision to leave everything behind and drive hundreds of miles to an unfamiliar place. I wanted to spill every last bean, but his enthusiastic command to follow stole my words.

I trailed him into the restaurant, surprised to find so many people squished in booths. They were all factory workers, judging by their matching blue jumpsuits. Cody led us toward the back to a lonely two-seater and clapped his hands.

"It's been too long since I've been here. I'm going to recommend the chicken or the catfish. The skirt steak is good too. Oh, and—"

"How about you get one thing, I'll get another and we share?" I suggested.

He quieted, and I could see the wheels in his mind turning. "Sounds good. I'll do the catfish, you do the chicken."

I kept the joke concerning dessert to myself, hiding it behind my smile. The waitress arrived promptly and took our orders. Cody kept her at the table with endless chatter, but she seemed delighted.

"If the chef has time, tell him Cody is here," he said.

"Sure thing."

When she was gone, I inquired, "Is there anyone you don't know?"

He scratched his chin and glanced at the ceiling. "I met the president once…."

Cocking a brow, I teased, "Which one?"

He blinked at me as if my question was misplaced. "Clinton, Bush, and Obama."

He proceeded to go into how he'd first met Bill Clinton on a first-grade field trip, which had sparked his curiosity about politics. Apparently he had gone around the classroom with a petition to make homework illegal. I should have known better than to ask questions, but I loved Cody's voice.

"You've had too many adventures for one person."

"I know, right? But we're on an adventure together now. Seriously, though. I'm going to have back issues by the time I'm thirty due to all those books they made us lug home."

I sputtered a laugh, completely agreeing with the man. When the waitress returned with our drinks, he quieted and traced the rim of his water glass.

Feeling playful, I teased, "This must be a record for you. A whole minute without talking?"

He looked at me with those big blue eyes. His bottom lip went between his teeth for an instant. "You're not the first to say that."

"Honestly, I don't mind. Like I said before, it's nice to have someone to talk to."

"Yeah, but I'm sure your ears are buzzing by now."

"Pleasantly so."

I didn't miss the flash of heat in his eyes as he peeled away the paper wrapping and struck the straw in the corner of his mouth, his jaw ticking. Remembering his earlier confession that anxiety aggravated his condition, I wondered if I had inadvertently hit a nerve.

"So how do you know this Albie Smith?" I asked, wanting to break the tension.

He instantly perked up. "Albie has been feeding the locals for years and opened his doors for meetings with the factory workers, way back when. He'd bake pies and cookies while we drafted the petition... oh my God, Aiden. His apple pie... don't tell my mom, but it's better than hers."

I mimicked his zipped-lips motion, drawing a bashful smile out of him.

"I wish I could get out here more often."

Our meals arrived promptly, and the moment the chicken hit my mouth, I moaned in bliss. Cody offered me a piece of his fish, and I took it from his fork, throwing him a heated look that made him wiggle. I'd never been so flirtatious before, especially in public. Brian had always told me I needed to loosen up a bit, but being open where people could see unnerved me... but being so far from home, I felt free. I supposed it had a lot to do with Cody—the guy was seriously the captain of easygoing.

"Are we still in Montana? This tastes like it should come out of some fancy New York restaurant," I said, devouring my meal.

"Oh yeah. Albie is good like that. I told him he should go on one of those cooking competitions. He'd so win, but he told me he prefers peace and quiet as opposed to fame and fortune." He took a sip of his water, then inquired, "Have you been to New York?"

"I have a place there, yes. My job has me traveling a lot, but their main office is out of the city, so I spend some time there."

"That's cool. I got as close as DC. One day I'll make it to the Big Apple. My uncle Rob has been there three times, the lucky bastard."

"Who is a lucky bastard?" a man asked as he stepped up to the table. Judging by his crisp white shirt and apron, I assumed this was the chef Cody had requested to visit our table. He was younger than I would have thought—early thirties perhaps. He must have been fresh out of culinary school because he looked the part, but having tasted his work, I would have thought him to be older.

Cody gasped and shot to his feet. "You, for having the pleasure of being in my company."

The chef laughed as they hugged, Cody patting him on the back. When he was back in the booth, the man nodded to me.

"Introduce me to your friend?"

"Right! Albie, this is Aiden, all the way from Texas. We are on a quest to find a lost relative of his," Cody explained.

"Nice to meet you," I said cordially and accepted his hand.

"Enjoying your food?" he asked.

"Absolutely! It's amazing," I said. "It was a pleasant surprise."

"Good. I try."

"While we're here… did you or anyone you know live in the Garden by chance?" Cody asked.

The man cocked a brow. "The Garden? No."

"So you're not related to a Thomas Smith that resided at 1103 Orange Blossom Drive?"

Albie looked around for a moment, then said softly, "I'm not really from around here, but don't tell anyone I said that. I will deny it."

Cody chuckled. "You wanted by the law, my friend? Is that it?"

"Not exactly. I just like to keep a low profile." He shrugged, but something dark crossed his face.

"Wait… you are serious?" Cody said, the disbelief in his voice thick.

"Yes. Can I ask why you thought I was related to this Thomas Smith?"

"Similar names."

Albie covered his laugh. "Cody, my friend, I love you. You know that, right?"

Cody sighed good-naturedly. "I know it was a long shot, but every angle must be explored."

"Okay, Detective Bannar."

"Besides, I figured it was a hell of an excuse to drive out here," Cody said.

"Thank you, president of my fan club. You can always try Jeff Smith, who lives in Bradbury," Albie suggested, his expression turning amused.

"Bradbury? Where is that?" I asked, my interest heightened.

"South of Valley Forge, about an hour," Cody said, slumping.

Chuckling, Albie clapped Cody on the shoulder. "I better get back. It was nice to see you again."

When the man was gone, I returned my attention to Cody, who was frowning at his empty plate. "I get too excited sometimes and don't think things through. Sorry if I dragged you out here for nothing."

"Are you kidding?" I huffed. "The food was amazing and the company enthralling."

He instantly perked up, his smile splitting his face, and I wanted to drag him into the bathroom for a little suck-face.

"Well, we do have some names at least," he said.

I nodded, disheartened that he had changed the conversation so quickly. His hand coming down on my own startled me, and I gazed into his luminous eyes.

"I forgot to ask you earlier! I'm getting together with some friends tonight, and I'd like you to come. Nothing major, just a few drinks. I want you to meet them. Please? It will be fun, guaranteed."

How could I say no to those puppy-dog eyes? "Okay."

He made a sound of supreme joy, then rubbed his palms together. "Dessert?"

I grinned, keeping my desire to myself, and shared a piece of apple pie with him. I was surprised to find I was looking forward to meeting Cody's friends.

CHAPTER TEN

AS THE sun slowly sunk into the west, I rocked on my feet in front of my motel room. I was in a weird mood, caught between looking forward to the night and forcing myself to brood about it. I came here to find someone, not party, but Cody made it impossible to not want to spend time with him. He was right about one thing—I could use a little more fun, and I tried to feel up about our night out, but I thought I should be miserable with all the crap going on in my life.

My father had left several none-too-polite messages, which I promptly sent to the trash bin. I knew I needed to deal with it eventually, but I wasn't in the mood to listen to him insult me again. I didn't completely trust myself to remain calm and not say something I knew I'd regret later. Pushing my disapproving parental figure aside, I couldn't help being excited to hang out with Cody.

Wait… was this a date? He hadn't explicitly asked me out in the traditional sense, but I got the feeling he had wanted to. I wasn't sure how to feel about it, considering I wouldn't be in Valley Forge much longer, but spending time with Cody was highly welcome, date or not. I had yet to figure out why I was so attracted to him, but I didn't question it.

A gorgeous Ford Cobra turned into the parking lot, hard music vibrating outward. When it pulled up next to me, I looked around in confusion. Maybe they were looking for directions?

The rear door opened, and Cody stuck his head out. "Come on."

The moment of shock passed, and I managed to get my feet moving, scooting in so I was smashed between the door and Cody. When I was settled, several sets of faces turned to regard me, their interested smiles unnerving me.

"Hi?" I stumbled.

"Oh, guys, this is Aiden, the dude I was telling you about. Aiden, these are my friends...," Cody said, running through the names so quickly I had a hard time keeping up.

The driver, Jarome, smiled at me, his bright white teeth making an appearance. "Any old friend of C-man is a new friend of mine."

Introductions aside, he cranked the music back up and peeled rubber, the force sending me against the seat. Several conversations started up, and I reminded myself to breathe, the air stuffy and musky with the scent of pot.

Cody turned to me and leaned in, his arms stretching along the back of the seat, but he didn't touch me. "Sorry. It's a little cramped."

His minty breath brushed across me, and I remembered what his mouth felt like against mine. Despite wanting to get a little frisky with him, I wanted to relax and not have to worry about what to say when it came time for me to leave.

"Aiden? Sorry, when I said a few friends... well, I don't have just a few friends—"

"That would definitely be an understatement," I cut in.

He laughed, his cheeks pulling up to crease the corners of his eyes. It quickly died, and he looked away for a moment before asking, "Did I make you uncomfortable?"

The disappointed look in his eyes stilled me. I shook my head. "No, it's just a 'strange town, strange people' kind of thing. It's not your fault."

He sighed visibly, his shoulders slumping. "Good. I can be overzealous sometimes, but I don't mean to. Just tell me to back off if I do."

"Okay." Looking at the window, I said loud enough for him to hear me, "But I've enjoyed everything we've done so far."

I kept my eyes on the passing houses, but I knew from his gasp that he'd gotten my hint. I knew I shouldn't encourage this... thing between us, but damn it, I wanted more despite my reservations. Cody didn't say anything the rest of the drive, the rap music vibrating deep into my bones. I had never been one for such music, but I found myself enjoying cruising in a sweet car with badass lyrics spilling out.

We pulled into a parking lot, and Jarome killed the engine. Everyone filed out, and I was glad to be back on my feet. I couldn't believe six people had been squished into the car. Cody smiled at me, but his expression was guarded.

"Ready for some fun?"

"You know what? I am."

"Good. Because fun is my occupation," he teased as we headed toward a bar.

"Maybe I should purchase stock. Sounds very lucrative."

He laughed, his joy enveloping me. My stomach did some weird tumbly thing as I took in every inch of his happiness. What I wouldn't do to be so carefree.

When we were inside, I inhaled, pulling the scent of alcohol and cigarettes deep into my lungs. Any other time I'd be repulsed, but all I could smell was fun. We took our places at a table, and Cody handed me a drink menu.

"They have excellent mixed drinks. I recommended the Long Island unless you're a beer kind of guy," Cody said. "The piña colada is good too. Oh, and—"

"What are you having?" I inquired.

He frowned and looked at his menu.

Jarome laughed. "We usually take bets on what C-man is going to have this week."

"I limit myself to one alcoholic beverage a week. I love my liver too much," Cody said.

"You can't get drunk like that." A guy with long, braided hair snickered, his lids speckled with silver glitter.

"That's the point," Cody replied, his tone unusually dark. He turned to me and shrugged. "I'll have what you're having."

I turned my attention to the menu, scrutinizing the choices. I settled for something not guaranteed to knock Cody on his ass with one shot. He seemed pleased with my choice. He collected everyone's drink orders, Jarome opting for a plain soda, then moseyed up to the bar.

The guy with the glittered lids scooted next to me, his chocolate eyes doing a once-over on me. "My man does like his music. With all the commotion I didn't get to properly introduce myself. I'm DeShawn. So how long you two been together?"

I was completely caught off guard by the assumption that Cody's friends thought we were together, and I was hesitant to correct him. "Not long. I'm not from around here."

"Really?" Jarome interjected. "Because he wouldn't shut up about you."

DeShawn burst out in laugher. "Seriously, babe? When does Cody shut up about anything?"

They snickered, and I couldn't help agreeing. "How long have you two known him?"

"Since high school," Jarome spoke up, scooting closer. "He made quite a splash for a little freshman."

"Oh yeah," another guy said, sliding to my other side, his hazel eyes bright with amusement. "I'm Mark. But that is nothing compared to the night he was crowned prom king."

"What?" I croaked and glanced at Cody, who was busy chatting with the bartender, his hands going a million miles as he illustrated some story or another.

"All the girls were in love with him—"

"And boys," DeShawn interjected.

I tried to imagine Cody in a suit, a fake crown on top his head, waving around a plastic wand but couldn't see it, and not because he wasn't the jock type.

"It wasn't his idea, though," Jarome said. "Running for prom king—"

"Jarome," DeShawn chastised, his tone harsh.

The man looked down meekly. "Well, you'll have to ask him about it."

As the group quieted, I realized something unpleasant had happened, and I found myself wanting to know desperately. The question was poised on the tip of my tongue, but I wasn't going to force them to reveal sensitive information.

"He took the crown from me, you know," Mark said, chuckling. "My girlfriend was pissed. Her perfect idea of a perfect prom was shattered."

I looked at him, meaning to say something intelligent, but I failed. "You're not gay?"

Mark burst out in laughter. "What, a straight guy can't hang with queers?"

I blinked blankly at him, my cheeks warming. "I'm sorry. I didn't mean to—"

"You keep denying it all you want, baby. I know you powder your nose," DeShawn said.

"It's called tinted lotion," Mark bit back, his expression light. "I wasn't voted hottest guy for nothing."

I was so taken back by their light banter, my head hurt. Mark was an anomaly to me. I couldn't believe he so easily accepted that his friends were gay and was okay with hanging out with them—and dandy with people assuming he was gay as well.

Cody returned with a drink tray and set everyone's orders in front of them.

"About time. I thought I was going to perish from thirst," Jarome teased.

Cody beamed and nudged Mark out of the seat so he could sit next to me. He didn't hesitate to scoot close, his arm brushing my own. Though I enjoyed being close to him, he made me self-conscious. What if my breath stank? *This isn't a date*, I reminded myself. I needed to stop worrying about such things.

Taking a sip of his drink, Cody made a sound of delight. I watched the way his cheeks rose, how his throat shifted... the way his moistened lips shone in the light. I realized I wanted to kiss him again desperately, drag him off to a quiet corner—better yet, take him back to my motel room and peel his clothes from his body.

I knew he had a good body, but I wanted to see it bared to me. It got hot really quickly, and I took a big swig of my drink, hoping it would cool me off.

I resigned myself to watching the circle of friends, their chatter relaxing me, and Cody drew out a smile from me as he talked endlessly.

"What about you, Aiden?" Cody asked suddenly.

"Sorry, what?" I hadn't followed the conversation very closely, my attention on him.

"Who is on your top five?"

"My top five?" I asked dubiously, glancing at everyone.

"Oh come on, don't be shy," DeShawn burst out. "Sorry, Jarome, but I'd so leave you for Taylor Lautner. I don't pray often, but when I do, I pray he will become gay."

Jarome rolled his eyes as laughter bounced around me. After a moment, everyone's attention settled back on me.

"Ah... I don't really have one," I managed.

"I think he's a little shy," Cody said. "I've recently replaced my number one with Liam Neeson. I mean, do I need to explain?"

"Honey, he can *take* me anytime."

"I feel left out." Mark sulked, finishing off his beer.

Cody slipped out of his stool and hugged the man close, ruffling his hair.

The guy laughed. "Cut it out."

A man walked up to our table and peered at Cody's drink, the bar lights highlighting his auburn hair. "Looks like I lost the bet."

Gasping, Cody hugged the guy. "Fuck, man. Where have you been?"

"Down, boy. I've been busy."

"I know!" Cody shouted. "Hey, this is Aiden. I'm helping him with some stuff. Aiden, this is Wylie. He's not from around here either, but he visits us a lot. We miss him when he is not around."

Cody went on, detailing their friendship and how Wylie had organized a fundraiser for some politician. I shook Wylie's hand, and he pulled up a seat next to Cody. I was amazed that he had so many friends. Besides Brian, I'd only had one other friend that I would consider close, and that was up for debate. I shouldn't be surprised. Cody was the type of person everyone wanted to be around.

"Remind me to get you a chew toy for Christmas to keep that mouth busy," Wylie teased, then winked at me. "You might want to invest in earplugs."

"Hey, are you going to give us a dance for the fundraiser?" DeShawn inquired.

A gentle blush crept up Wylie's cheeks, and he chuckled. "I'm playing management this time around. Maybe next time."

Everyone seemed crestfallen at the news.

Turning to Wylie, Cody asked, "So who is number one on your top five list?"

Clearing his throat, Wylie reached into his pocket and fiddled with his phone. He held it out, and I leaned in to get a better view. I grinned, recognizing the guy. I wasn't going to say it out loud, but I'd jacked off to his image once or twice.

"Golf's bad boy? Fuck... he's my number six," Cody commented. "Hey, didn't he go to your college or something?"

The man glanced at Cody, then shrugged and pocketed his phone. "I think so."

The time passed, conversations filling the hours, Cody fetching drinks. I accepted a second round but passed on a third. DeShawn giggled at something Jarome said, his lips pressing a kiss on DeShawn's lobe. I was amazed at the openness and looked around, but the patrons seemed oblivious to the show of affection.

Different place, I reminded myself. I couldn't help picturing Bibby and Georgie in place of Jarome and DeShawn. No doubt they'd be fearless. It was a lovely thought, and I aspired to the freedom being comfortable with oneself brought.

Cody punched his fist in the air as Semisonic's "Closing Time" filled the bar. I shook my head as they started singing along, rocking with the melody. Cody wrapped an arm around my shoulders and urged me to follow the flow. I obeyed, my cheeks hurting as I grinned.

Wylie suddenly broke from the crowd and pulled his phone out, then pressed it to his ear. After a moment, his expression dropped, and he retreated to a quiet corner.

Leaning close so I could hear, Cody said, "He's a busy boy. Who knew fundraising is so much work? I mean, all the planning… venues, food, tickets, and raffles. I respect the dude, though."

"I'm sorry, but I have to cut out," Wylie said, his eyes wide as if he had received bad news. "I'll see everyone around, okay?"

Cody hugged the man, and then Wylie was gone as quickly as he had appeared. The night wound down, DeShawn falling asleep against his boyfriend and Mark looking beyond buzzed.

Cody turned to me and winked. "You ready to leave?"

"Yeah." It was strange, but I wanted the night to continue.

By the time we got back to the motel, it was well after midnight, and I was surprised how quickly time had flown by. When I was back on my feet, I stretched, the cool night air getting into my lungs and waking me up.

Cody smiled. "I hope you had fun."

"I did. It was nice meeting your friends."

"Yeah, they are good peeps." Glancing at my door, he said, "Anyway, we'll pick up the search tomorrow."

I nodded, biting my lip. I had to force the words out, but Cody's hesitation to leave fueled me. "You want to… come in for a bit?"

"I'd like that." He turned and waved to the car.

"Oh, get some!" DeShawn yelled, his words slurred.

Cody flushed and ushered me into my room. When we were inside, I berated myself for leaving a pair of dirty boxers on the floor and scrambled to push them under the bed. Awkwardly, I inquired if he wanted something to drink.

"Sure. What you got?"

I looked at him. "Water."

He chuckled, his eyes twinkling in the low light of the room. "That's okay."

We stood there for several long seconds, and I wanted to strip him naked and push him on the bed, but I was afraid of the intimacy that was developing between us. Still, I was desperate to be close to him.

"Can I show you something?" I blurted.

He tried to hide a salacious grin.

"No, I mean… the real reason I'm here."

"Oh."

"Not that I don't want to…. But I—I haven't been honest with you," I stumbled, my stomach in knots. At his quizzical look, I reached under the bed and pulled out the footlocker. I selected a handful of Bibby's letters. I cradled them in my hands for a moment, then offered them to him.

He accepted them, a frown arching over his lips. I watched him as he took a seat on the mattress and started reading, his eyes sliding over the words. He sunk into the bed, his attention completely on the letters, the paper shaking as if his hand quaked. It seemed like hours as he went through several, but he finally looked up, his eyes shiny with unshed tears.

"Christ, Aiden. This is beautiful."

My mouth fell open in response, but I couldn't find any words. I had expected him to tease me about driving several states away to find some guy I'd never known. But I shared his sentiment regarding Bibby's letters.

"No one writes like this anymore," he said softly, running his thumb across the paper. "This is… amazing. Where did you find them?"

"In my mother's attic," I said. "Georgie was my great-uncle."

Cody licked his lips and carefully folded a letter. "Did you ask your mom if she knows Bibby?"

"She didn't," I said, heat coursing through me at the lie.

After a moment he wiped his eyes dry. "Look what you did to me."

"I like the center of my chocolate-chip cookie gooey," I said before I could stop myself and made a face. "Sorry, that was really stupid."

He laughed. "Better than some of my pick-up lines."

Taking a deep breath, Cody rose to his feet and gently set the letters on the table. "You're here looking for this Bibby because...?"

"Yes. I... I have my reasons."

"I'm assuming there are envelopes?"

"Yeah." I said, plucking an envelope from the chest.

"Wow! There's more?" He gasped, his eyes widening at the stacks of letters.

"I haven't gone through them all yet, but there are several years' worth." I handed him the envelope.

"Orange Blossom Drive.... Alice Barrington? The surname listed on here wasn't in any of the public records," Cody said.

"I know, which was why I wasn't so surprised when we came up empty."

Stroking his chin, he muttered, "I think it's obvious Bibby was a nickname. I mean back then, two guys was... they would be shunned. Aliases made sense. Aiden, this is so much better than looking for sunken ships or lost jewelry. We have to find Bibby.... God, can you imagine the stories he might tell?"

I nodded, feeling strangely light. It felt good being truthful with him, and what was better, he didn't seem to think I was foolish. Sullenly, I said, "You realize the chances of Bibby still being alive are none to negative?"

He blinked at me. "Did you consider that when you drove up here?"

"Point taken," I said.

He smiled and shrugged. "We have to find him... or his grave."

"So you're still in?"

"I was never out," he countered.

"Okay. We know he used an alias, and I'm betting he never lived on Orange Blossom Drive."

He snapped his fingers. "Maybe he had the return letters sent to a close friend. But if this Alice Barrington is the friend, why isn't she listed in the records?"

I nodded. "That's a good question. She could have rented the place or the owners were friends of hers. I don't know. Maybe going through the rest of the letters might uncover something."

It was as if someone had jammed a needle in my arm and injected me with liquid excitement. My stomach tumbled, my heart pounded hard, and Cody's enthusiasm fueled my own. As the gears turned in his head, his smile slowly split his face.

"We have to find the person who lived at this address during the years these letters were written. Chances are that's the friend or they knew Alice Barrington. But…."

"But?"

"It's late," he said and yawned.

"Yeah, first thing in morning?"

"You bet your pants."

After a long moment of grinning at each other, Cody looked around the room. "I assumed we were going to… I don't have a ride home."

I blushed. "I wanted to…. *Want to*. Just… you don't have to leave. The bed is big enough for the both of us."

His smile was lovely, and his eyes sparkled as they settled on the bed. I knew what was running through his mind, because thoughts of being so close to him were busy in mine too. But it was late and I was tired, and Cody did something to me I wasn't comfortable examining at the moment. I was terrified getting intimate with him again would exacerbate those emotions.

"Just sleep," he confirmed.

I nodded. I took the bathroom first, washing up and brushing my teeth. I hesitated to get undressed and decided to leave my clothes on.

When I emerged, he was sitting on the bed, eying the footlocker as if he wanted to dive right in. Turning his attention to me, he asked, "Mind if I use your toothpaste?"

"No, go ahead. There's a fresh brush in there too."

"I know. Gigi is good like that."

Cody passed me and closed the door behind him. I took a deep breath and slowly let it out. Telling someone the truth of what I was doing up here had released a boatload of stress, and having a plan of action put everything in perspective. Plus, it was nice sharing this adventure together.

He returned a moment later, dressed in nothing but a pair of boxers with the Road Runner printed across them. How appropriate, I thought. Cody was the Road Runner of conversations. When I found the hints of a tattoo peeking over the waistband, my brows rose.

He gasped. "Want to see?"

I cleared my throat, not sure how to answer that.

He pushed the fabric down to reveal a devil's face, a wicked grin leering out at me.

"That's so you," I said.

"I know, right? I'm pretty on the outside, but inside I'm a little demon." He winked. "Anyway. I usually sleep naked, but I didn't want to—ah, you're not going to bed like that, are you?"

I glanced at my clothes, feeling as if I were bundled for winter. "I didn't want to...."

"I forgot. You're shy." He made his way to the bed and pushed the sheets back.

Sighing, I pushed my jeans down my legs and discarded them. I left my T-shirt on, figuring progress was progress, and pensively approached the mattress. When we were settled, I wanted to roll over and hold him close, not for sex but comfort. It took me a long time to fall asleep, my mind replaying the day's events.

Cody's little snore didn't help either. I quickly learned that even asleep, he was a talker.

CHAPTER ELEVEN

I CAME awake slowly, something warm and solid up against me. As my sight sharpened, I shot up, startled. Cody was facing me, his smile bright, his thumb racing as he texted on his phone.

"About time, you bum," he said.

"Oh…. Right."

As memories of last night swirled around me, I relaxed. It had been a long time since I'd shared Zs with someone, and it was strange sleeping with them, no sex involved. It was kind of nice. I got up and made directly for the bathroom to relieve myself and brush my teeth. When I returned, Cody was still in bed texting furiously, his face twisted in excitement.

When he noticed me, he pushed his phone into his pocket, and I realized he was dressed. "Aiden… I know we said we'd get started in the morning, but Christmas is only a few days away, and there is something very important I need to do. I almost forgot."

"I understand."

Sitting up, he beamed. "And you're coming with me."

"I am?"

"I'm not going to let you sit here in this room and rot. Get dressed, because we are going Christmas shopping!"

"Okay," I said, not at all disheartened to be sidetracked. "So I take it I'm driving?"

"I forgot about that. Do you mind?"

"Nope."

"We have to go back to my place, though, so I can change. I smell like beer."

"Not a problem."

As I threw some clothes on, I couldn't believe it was only a few days until Christmas. That thought sobered me. Had Mom been alive, her house would have been decked out, every inch of the porch, every tree and shrub glowing with lights and the smell of pine thick throughout the house. And the dinner she would have made…. I closed my eyes, remembering last year. It had only been us and Mrs. Johnson from down the street, but it had been perfect. We had shared some wine, getting a little buzz on as I told her about the cities I'd seen.

"Aiden?"

"Sorry," I said, offering Cody a smile. "I was just thinking about the holidays."

"I love Christmastime! The food and the decorations and the snow. Oh, and the gifts. I usually go broke around this time of the year," he said, pushing his feet into his shoes. "Of course, receiving is just as much fun. Unless it's underwear. My great-aunt Mildred still insists on getting me tighty-whities a size too small, even though I've told her I'm a boxers kind of guy. She doesn't understand that the boys need to breathe, you know?"

As he droned on, I smiled to myself. If I'd had half the balls—pun intended—Cody did in letting his thoughts be known, I might not be in this mess.

Cody gasped and shot to his feet. "What was the one thing you wanted when you were a kid but never got?"

"Ah… a Dr. Dreadful Lab."

"Oh, the laboratory where you make body parts out of goo and eat them? That's awesome! I remember that."

Feeling light, I inquired, "What about you? What did you want?"

His cheeks colored. "You'll think I'm weird."

"I've found that I kind of like your brand of weird."

He gave me the most dazzling smile. "For two years straight, I begged Mom for a Ken doll, the Hawaiian one. My sisters would force me to play dolls with them all the time, and I was tired of playing Stacie, so I figured if I had my own boy doll… well. I was a kid. Of course, by the time my parents finally gave in, my sisters outgrew Barbie. I think I still have him packed away somewhere.

When I was thirteen I started mashing him together with my brother's G.I. Joe."

"Christ, my father would have murdered me if he found me playing with—" I realized what I was saying and cut off my words, but something crossed over Cody's face. "Anyway. We should get going. Long lines and stuff."

"Right." His smile was thin, and I knew he wanted to ask about my personal life, but I wasn't ready to talk about all my problems. I was having too much fun with this guy to let the gloom ruin it.

It took us a good hour to get out of his house, Marge making us sit down and eat some breakfast. After she handed Cody a wad of cash and her shopping list, we were off in Cody's car. He talked some more about his favorite toys, especially the toy drive he helped with every year and how he dressed up as Santa's little helper.

"I could definitely see you as an elf," I teased, running my eyes all over him.

He laughed, then patted his stomach. "Not enough gut for Santa."

It amazed me how easy it was to joke with him. I'd never bantered like this with Brian. Cody took us across town and turned into a large mall with several big chain stores. Our first stop was Toys"R"Us, and as we walked inside, a giddiness vibrated through me, one I hadn't experienced in a long time.

"Look at all this shiny stuff," he said, then unfolded a paper.

"Let's do girls first, because if we do boys, I'll never want to leave."

I followed him, weaving around people as they rushed to fill their carts.

"Okay," Cody said, pointing at a play set of little groceries with *kawaii* faces. "That is kinda cute."

The cart started to fill up quickly, and when we turned into the boys' section, his face lit up like a Christmas tree. I had to admit, I wanted to make right for the Spider-Man action figures. I couldn't recall a time when I'd been in a toy store. Mostly, I had resigned myself to admiring toys from afar. Dad had always considered things like comics and Play-Doh a waste of money and time.

"You have a big family, huh?" I commented as more things went into the cart.

"You have no idea," Cody said, moving the jaw of a T-Rex up and down. "Thirteen nieces and nephews… they get expensive. But I love seeing their faces when they open my gifts. They all know I'm the king of gift giving. How about you? Any siblings?"

"An older sister, but we don't talk much. I do have a newborn nephew, but they live in California."

Turning to me, Cody frowned. "That's it?"

I shrugged.

"UPS is cheaper for shipping big boxes, you know. Spoil them, I say."

"Her husband has got that covered." At his quizzical look, I added, "She married a lawyer. The ring he got her is probably worth as much as my mother's farmhouse."

His eyes lit up. "Perfect. You can get him a *Where's Waldo* tie."

"They make that?"

"Sure."

I shook my head, trying to imagine Scott in an expensive suit and a noisy tie. "I don't really know him."

"That makes me sad."

"Why?"

"Because the holidays are about family and friends, and you seem to have little."

I didn't know how to respond to that, so I didn't say anything.

"Sorry. I hit a nerve."

"No, you're right. What little family I do have doesn't want anything to do with me."

He stopped again and searched my face, his eyes impossibly warm. "Can I ask why?"

I sighed, looking away. I wanted to brush him off, but Cody had a way of making me feel better. After a long moment I said, "They don't approve of my choices."

"Oh, that," he murmured. "That's hard."

"Yeah," I agreed. "On the bright side, I don't have to worry about an avalanche of 'two sizes too small' tighty-whities."

He smiled, but it couldn't hide the emotion, and it warmed me that this guy who hardly knew me could feel sad on my account.

"Well, I think we got everything on the list."

I looked at the pile of toys in the cart. "Looks that way."

We spent a good hour in checkout, the line stretching down the aisle. Cody chatted lightly, reminiscing about being a kid. I focused on the sound of his voice, the excitement shining in his eyes, and couldn't help feeling envious of his life. My childhood had been okay, but the constant worry that Dad might not approve of something or other had shadowed my every move.

After dumping everything into his car, we made our way to a department store, and I threw some spare change into the Salvation Army canister. Cody deposited a five-dollar bill. I wondered if I should get him something for Christmas. He'd been so kind to me and seemed determined to help me in any way possible.

"Do you think they ever went Christmas shopping together?" he said as he fingered a sweater.

There was no need to explain who *they* were. "I'd like to believe they did."

Cody loaded the cart with clothes and ties. He arched a playful brow at me, then pressed a Domo-kun tie against my chest. I waved it away, and he chuckled.

"Am I wrong to presume you will still be in town for Christmas?" he asked, his voice quaking.

"More than likely."

"Good. You're invited for Christmas dinner."

"I don't want to intrude—"

"Really?" he scoffed. "After meeting my family and friends, you're going to say that?"

"Point taken."

"Perfect. We need to get you a Christmas sweater, then. It's a requirement. Mom's rules."

I arched a brow at him.

He led me right to the holiday sweater section and began riffling through the stacks. He gasped, then held one up.

I sneered at the sweater he chose. "It's hideous."

"I know. Isn't it great?"

I shook my head but accepted his pick. Our last stop of the day was a pet store, where Cody dropped two hundred dollars on several new vests for Fabio, chew toys, and Christmas-themed rawhides. He talked about how skinny and matted the little guy had been, and Cody was determined to spoil him rotten to make up for his shitty start in life.

"Well, I think we got everyone's lists covered."

"What about the naughty list?" I asked.

He froze in the process of stuffing his car to blink at me wide-eyed. I cleared my throat awkwardly but said nothing. I didn't know why I said it, but there was no taking back my suggestion.

After a moment, he exhaled as if he'd been holding his breath. "I thought you'd never ask. I mean… you want—?"

"Yes," I said loudly, then turned away, my cheeks flaming.

Cody surprised me by spinning me around and pecking my lips. Heat exploded across my skin, and I looked around so see if anyone was watching. His hand on mine startled me, the touch whisper soft.

"No one cares," he said.

"Sorry, I'm not used to… yes. I very much want to again."

He slumped his shoulders. "Phew. I thought I sucked."

"Are you kidding?"

"Well, I didn't want to push you, and you seemed reluctant… it doesn't matter now. So you want to sit on Santa's lap, do you?"

I sputtered a laugh, the thought of being naughty with him waking me up. "Yeah. I want Santa to tell me all about the things he has in his sack."

Cody grinned salaciously. "Never mind that. Santa-brand candy canes are the best."

I glanced at his car. "The motel?"

"No, my place."

"Ah, a little noisy?"

"No, I mean my place. You'll see," he said, his lips quirking up into a secretive smirk.

"Okay."

BY THE time we got back to the Bannar farmhouse it was late, the sun dipping behind the mountains. He turned into the driveway but pulled around to the back and followed a dirt road. As we angled around the cattle fence, a little house came into view.

"It used to be a rooming house for farmhands. Dad converted it to an apartment a few years ago. Now it's mine," he said, then looked askance at me. "So we'll be alone. I do have a roommate, but he's at work right now."

"Okay," I muttered, trying to quell the excitement bouncing around my insides.

He killed the engine and got out, and I followed.

"I usually stuff all the presents in my closet so no one can find them, but we can do that later," he said, a smile pulling at the corner of his lips.

When we were inside I stopped for an instant, taken aback by the modern look of his place. The light color of the pinewood contrasted perfectly with all the dark-burnished furniture and glass tables. Cody seemed to have inherited his father's love for rocks. A geode was displayed on the table, its crystals reflecting the light.

"Wow."

"You like it?"

"You got a nice place going on here," I praised.

"This is just the wrapping paper. You haven't seen what's inside yet."

I arched a brow at him, and he tipped his head to the side. I followed him into his bedroom, and it was as if I'd just walked into another place and time. Posters of various bands lined the walls, and an electric guitar sat quietly in a corner. It reminded me of my room when I had been going through my rebellious stage.

I heard him close the door behind me, and my cock thumped in my pants.

"Do you want anything to drink?" he inquired, plucking a soda from a minifridge.

"No, I'm fine." I dropped my eyes to his computer desk, where a camera sat on a pedestal. "Is this where you film most of your videos?"

"Ah, yeah," he said, sticking a stubby pencil in the corner of his mouth. "I do a lot of filming around town too. Especially in summer. And sometimes I interview people. But this is where most of the magic happens. I just drape a sheet behind, so it looks somewhat professional."

The sound of wood cracking caught my attention, and I pointed at my own lips. Cody cursed and tossed the demolished pencil in a trash can.

"Sorry. I don't realize I do it sometimes. Especially when I'm—"

Nervous, I finished for him silently. It excited me to know I affected him so much.

"I'll be right back," he said.

"Okay."

When Cody disappeared into the bathroom, I sighed and plopped on his bed. I was as terrified as he was, and I had no idea why. As the water came on, I toed my shoes off and brushed my thumb across my erection. It was a long time before he finally emerged. He came to stand in front of me, his expression hopeful, but his movements were uncoordinated.

"Are you sure you don't want something to drink?"

I dug my fingers into his shirt and pulled. He followed, and I wrapped my arm around his waist, then spanned his stomach with my palm, his skin hot and smooth. His gasp was lovely, and I urged his shirt up his body and over his shoulders. As I pressed my lips to his abdomen in a soft kiss, his fingers dug into my scalp, pulling gently.

I glanced up to find him watching me intently, his eyes hooded, his lips parted.

Feeling playful, I asked, "Do I get to sample Santa's candy cane now?"

Beaming, he popped the button on his jeans, and I didn't waste a second. I pushed his pants down his legs, desperate to see him in all his naked glory. His boxers quickly followed, and the moment his cock was freed, I sank to my knees and planted a kiss along the side of the shaft. He hissed, and I flattened my tongue against the length, licking my way to the glans as if it were indeed a candy cane. I cupped his ass and used it for support as I took his dick into my mouth, tracing the wrinkles with my tongue.

"Oh... fuck," he whispered harshly.

I popped his cock out of my mouth and grinned. "I see you weren't overestimating the quality of Santa-brand candy canes."

He burst out in laughter, his body shaking. I repeated the motion, tonguing the glans, drawing out a shocked sigh. I licked every inch, slicking him, teasing, my palm cradling his balls.

"Aiden…. Jesus… slow down."

I backed off, not wanting him to come yet. "Can I ask something of you?"

He leaned in and pressed me down to the bed to straddle me, his body heat soaking through my clothes and deep down to my bones. His weight was perfect above me.

"Tell me what you need," he said, his voice dark.

Sandwiched between the plush duvet and his flushed body, I was powerless before him. I wanted to tell him things I'd never told anyone—not even Brian.

"Whatever you want," he said and planted a kiss on my neck. "Foot fetish? No problem. I wash my feet regularly."

I couldn't help it, I burst out in gut-splitting laughter. When I came down, I looked up into his amused smile. "I can't imagine I've done anything to give away something like that. So it makes me wonder what you're hiding."

His blush was lovely. "No, that's not… I just mean that I'm pretty open about things. I won't think you're weird. Hell, its common knowledge that I am the very definition of weird, so yeah."

Taking a deep breath, I nodded. "Okay. My request isn't weird, I promise. I just wasn't sure how far you wanted to take this is all."

"That doesn't tell me what you want," Cody said.

"Point taken," I conceded, then smacked his ass. "I need you to fuck me. Hard."

His lips curled up to crinkle the corners of his eyes. "I can so do that."

I accepted his help as he urged my shirt over my head, then undid my jeans. He got a good grip on my pants, then yanked them off, my cock bouncing to attention. He came to rejoin me, our dicks meeting once again, his lips fusing with mine. He felt so good, I wanted to lock my limbs around him and never let him get away.

He was off me in an instant, and I skimmed my eyes down his body to settle on his ass as he rifled through a drawer. He turned and held up the box of condoms and lube. "Found it."

I grinned as he rejoined me in bed, our bodies mashing together, his arms pulling me close. He ran his fingers across my jaw, his eyes hooded. His hand quickly glided down my shoulder and across my hip, where he dipped his fingers into the crack of my ass. I closed my eyes as he teased my asshole, his lips pressing against my neck.

"How many licks does it take to eat Santa's candy cane?" he whispered.

"I guess we'll have to find out."

Cody pushed me onto my back, and he parted my legs with his hips. It felt so good to be close to another man with nothing between us. Guiding my lips to his, I opened for him, and he took over the kiss. I followed his lead, responding to every sweep of his tongue. Cody was an amazing kisser. He swallowed my gasp as slick, cool fingers found my hole and smeared the lube. It had been too long since I'd had a cock inside me, and I let him know by thrusting into his touch.

Cody pulled away and sat up, his face bright as he sheathed himself with two condoms. "You're hot, and I don't want to come too fast."

His compliment did all kinds of nice things to me. I relaxed as I watched him settle between my legs and hook his arms behind my knees. His hips came flush against my ass, his cock pressing against my entrance. I forced myself to relax as he worked, rocking gently. The lube did its thing, Cody slipping into me. I'd always liked that initial push, the instant my ass was filled, the shock commanding all my attention.

"Okay?"

"Yeah," I rasped, concentrating on the way his girth filled me. It bordered on overwhelming, but that was because I hadn't done this for a while. My ass quickly adjusted, and he pushed forward until his balls made contact with my asscheeks. I grabbed the full globes of his butt, digging my fingers into his skin.

He withdrew slowly, then drove back in a long, smooth stroke. His attention remained on me, his eyes searching, his expression reading all carnal interest. As he repeated the motion, I dropped my head against the bed and sighed, relishing his presence. Cody sped up his strokes, every thrust expanding the pleasure until it engulfed me.

"Tell me what you need again, Aiden."

His words were erotic, the subtle authority arousing.

"I need you to fuck me hard. Please," I begged.

Cody thrust into me forcefully, his hips slapping against my ass, and I gasped. Before my brain could process the sensation, he started pounding me, and I lost all conception of time and reality. All that existed was him and his dick filling me, the sound of his breath, and the scent of his skin. I gripped my cock, squeezing securely, sure I would come from a single stroke. Cody was exactly what I needed, the sound of our bodies colliding driving me toward the edge at a million miles an hour.

"Phew," Cody whispered, slowing his strokes. "You are giving me a workout."

"Good. Will need it… after all those cookies, Santa…," I managed.

He laughed and dived back in, my moans filling the room anew. I'd never been this vocal before. His ass flexed beautifully in my palms as he drove into me over and over, his labored breath turning to quick gasps.

"I'm… close," he rasped.

I nodded, intending to let him know I was too, but I groaned instead as the pleasure fired off. Digging my nails into him, I growled, "Right there."

His grin was wolfish, and he threw my legs over his shoulders, then leaned in so my ass was off the bed. I lost my mind as he drilled me, his cock hitting my prostate with every thrust. Fireworks exploded around me, the tingle spreading throughout my body. I jerked my leaking cock, the orgasm shooting to the surface.

"Fuck!" I hissed as I came.

Cody barreled on as I erupted. He followed right behind me, thrusting as deep as he could go, his shouts of pleasure joining my own. Releasing my legs, he collapsed on top of me, our chests heaving with breath, our bodies slick with sweat.

"Holy shit," he muttered over and over.

I was too out of it to respond, the pleasure still riding me hard into the sunset, his cock still filling me. We stayed that way as his dick slowly deflated, our bodies molding together. His fingers ran through my hair, and I leaned into his touch.

"Let me clean up, and then we can cuddle," he said, withdrawing.

I grunted a response, too weary to do anything else. He was missed, and I focused on the sounds of Cody moving around in the bathroom. Something cold and rough shocked me, and I flipped my lids open to find him running a washcloth along my abdomen.

He grinned widely. "We made a mess."

Chuckling, I grappled him and pulled him back to bed. He didn't fight, wrapping his body around me, his lips finding my own.

We kissed passionately, every slow lick dazzling me, his hands running up and down my body.

"How did I do?" he whispered against my jaw.

I ran my nose across his neck, inhaling the scent of sex and sweat. "The best I've ever had."

"R-really?"

"Did I say that out loud?" I inquired, genuinely shocked.

"Yeah…. Really, though? Because you gave me a run for the moolah. Christ, it was better than a five-mile jog. You were awesome, by the way."

I hushed him, pulling him back to my lips. The sex had been amazing, but I realized I needed a heap load of cuddle time. He held me tenderly, his body warm and solid. Seconds stretched into minutes, a feeling of pure peace enveloping me.

"My mother died," I managed as I traced the rise of his abs.

"I'm sorry," he said, his tone reflecting true sorrow.

"She was hit by a car while taking a walk. I kept her on life support for five weeks, convinced she'd come out of it. I pulled the plug a few days before I came up here. I was trying to clean her house—*trying* being the operative word—when I found the letters. I can't understand why it was so hard to try and organize all her stuff. It's just lifeless things… not her. But I feel as if she's left a part of herself on everything. I don't know what I'm going to do. I wasn't prepared for this." I was aware the words were flowing from my lips, but it didn't seem real.

I moved to sit at the edge of the bed and proceeded to stare at the carpet. After a long moment, Cody joined me, his arms going around me, his chin resting on my shoulder. He didn't say anything, and I was glad for the comfort.

"I talked to her the day before the accident. She had called, and I told her I loved her, but that I was late for a meeting and that we'd talk soon."

"I'm sorry."

Frowning, I craned my neck to find Cody in tears.

He wiped them away and apologized again. "I'm my own waterworks plant."

Despite the heavy moment, I smiled. I pulled him back down to the bed and pressed my lips to his.

"Make me forget," I whispered.

CHAPTER TWELVE

"THAT ISN'T anything. Sophomore year, I dyed my hair rainbow, and it had nothing to do with gay pride," Cody said as he took a swig from the wineglass he had been nursing for the last hour. "Of course, I wasn't out at the time."

I smiled as Cody told me about all his high school adventures. In the back of my mind, I knew hours had flown by, the sky outside pitch-black. We had ordered pizza, and Cody had cracked open a cheap bottle of wine. We'd gone at it again, Cody taking me from behind until we were left in a puddle on his mattress. Having showered, we lay naked in bed, talking about everything and nothing.

"What about you? What was your rebellious stage like?" he inquired.

I propped my head against my palm and pushed my bottom lip out in thought. "I guess I skipped it."

"No way."

"I was always trying to please my father."

"Okay. Heavy subject. Do you want to pass on that?" he asked.

I thought for a moment. I was still surprised I had managed to talk about Mom, but now I had, I felt a little better. *Baby steps*, I told myself. "Yeah. Let's move on."

"Okay, I think I've run out of talking points for the night. Ask me something. Anything."

I cocked a dubious brow. "You? Out of talking points? I think you're lying. Either that or hell really has frozen over."

He giggled, the alcohol loosening him up. "Are you saying I have a big mouth?"

"Well… you know what they say. Big dick… big mouth."

"Shut up!" He hit me with a pillow. "No one ever said that."

I grinned. After a long moment, I inquired, "Can I ask about prom?"

His mood dropped, his easy expression bleeding away.

"I'm sorry. I shouldn't—"

"No, it's okay. I did say you can ask me anything."

"Your friends mentioned you being crowned prom king, but that it wasn't your idea," I said.

"What else did they say?"

"That you shattered Mark's girlfriend's dreams."

Cody smiled distantly, as if the memories were flashing before his eyes. He took a healthy swig, finishing off his glass, then set it on the bedside table. "Yeah. I'd only gone to take pictures for the school newspaper because Marcy was sick with mono. Despite being gay and accepted for the most part, it was still kind of weird to go to the prom with another guy back then, so I had planned to skip it, as I didn't have a date."

"Yeah. I didn't go at all."

"You didn't miss much. Anyway, someone entered me in the running for prom queen, but the principal quickly corrected it."

"Fuck. That's so unoriginal."

"I know, that's what I said. We all knew who it was, even if no one was willing to call him out. Long story short, I won by like two votes. Everyone cheered me on, but inside I felt... I don't know. I just wanted to run to the bathroom and bawl like a baby. Even though it hadn't turned into the big joke he'd intended, it hurt."

I sat up, my attention fully on Cody. "He?"

"Ryan Wychowski. My best friend since coming to live with Mom and Dad. We did everything together. But when I came out sophomore year... I don't know. He just couldn't handle it for some reason. I'm pretty sure his father being a bigoted asshole had something to do with it, but I tried to explain to him that I was still me. In the span of twenty-four hours, he went from my best friend to that *one*. The one kid you feared, that made you feel like shit. I know everyone has one, but I never imagined in a million years it would be him."

I scooted close and wrapped my arm around his shoulders. I didn't know what to say to make him feel better, so I kept my mouth shut, hating I'd dug up that pain. Cody rested his head against me, his arm going around my torso.

He sighed. "You feel nice."

After a long moment of holding him, I cursed. "I wish I was better at this."

He poked me in the side, making me chuckle. "You're doing fine. I never got over it and never will, but I've learned how to deal with it. I mean, I like to consider myself fucking lucky. I have parents and siblings who love me for me. And my friends... they've always been there."

He startled me by setting into action and straddling me. "And now I have you."

His declaration startled me. I opened my mouth to argue—

"Everyone says we are born alone and we die alone. I don't believe that. The people we meet in this life, the friends we make, the lovers we share ourselves with... we take that with us. I like to believe those memories are there when we finally kick it."

I didn't know what to say. I was sure I'd just been rocketed into space, Cody's words shaking my very foundation.

He kissed my lips, then got up, tossing the empty wine bottle in the trash. "Anyway. Life is too short to worry about the shit we can't change. Me, I like to devote all my energy to stuff I can fix. Which reminds me. I have to stop at the printer tomorrow and see if my T-shirts are done."

I was glad for the change of subject, that tightness in my head having returned for a brief moment. The sound of the front door closing startled us.

"I think that's my roommate," Cody said as he tossed my pants at me. "I want you to meet him. He could use a few more friends."

114

"Okay." I pushed my legs into my jeans, then looked around for my shirt, but Cody gripped my hand and pulled me along.

"Jules!" Cody exclaimed. "My man, how was work?"

The guy accepted Cody's hug. "Okay. Quiet, thankfully."

"Awesome," Cody said and turned to me. "Aiden, this is Jules. He's staying here for a little while. Jules, Aiden. I'm helping him track down a lost relative."

I accepted the man's hand, his expression friendly, if not a little weary. I felt strange making a new acquaintance looking and smelling like I'd just had sex. The man's eyes dipped down for an instant, as if he suspected what we had been doing.

"Aiden is from Texas," Cody added.

Jules nodded. "Nice to meet you. I hope you find what you're looking for."

"Thanks."

"I don't want to be rude, but I'm exhausted, so I'm going to head to bed."

"Okay, buddy. I stuck some pizza in your fridge if you get the munchies," Cody said.

Jules passed me a tight smile, then disappeared into a bedroom.

Cody leaned in, his voice low. "He's a little quiet."

I nodded. "Is he a high school friend?"

Cody pulled me back toward his bedroom. "No. He's in hiding."

I didn't inquire further as Cody guided me into bed. His grin was suggestive, and I returned the gesture.

"You don't mind sleeping here with me tonight, do you?"

"No, not at all."

We were naked in a flash, my head against his chest and his fingers in my hair. It all seemed so natural. I'd slept with Brian of course, but the times where we cuddled and talked into the wee hours of the morning had been far and few. If it wasn't early morning classes, then it was the fear of rumors going around. I could admit now, that hesitation was mostly on me. I was afraid my orientation would get out and back to my parents.

"You know what I think, Aiden?" Cody said after a while. "You need a little more fun in your life, and I know just the thing."

"Uh-oh," I teased.

"There's a benefit the day after Christmas. If you're still here, I'd like you to come. It's fifty bucks for dinner and music. Alcohol is extra. If that's okay? I can front you the money. It's for a good cause."

"I'm in." I didn't hesitate. "And I got it covered."

My body relaxed, the soreness setting in, and I fell asleep to Cody's lovely voice telling me all about his plans to dress as Santa this year.

CHAPTER THIRTEEN

"I'M STILL pissed with Josh's dad. I just want to strangle the man," Cody said, his attention on the road. "Unfortunately, political opinion is a protected right."

I smiled to myself. Cody had complained the past few days about not being able to get his T-shirt order. Apparently the guy who owned the printing shop refused to print a "hands up, don't shoot" design.

"But it's not like I don't know he is a bigot Republican." Cody smacked his lips then shrugged. "What are you going to do? Sorry, I'm being whiny again, aren't I?"

"It's okay."

He made an agitated sound as he unwrapped some gum and shoved it into his mouth.

"I mean really. Some people aggravate me to no end. Jesus preaches love and feed the poor, etcetera and etcetera. You'd think a 'devout Christian' like him would be more prolife... never mind. I'll hush."

I gripped his free hand, stroking his knuckles, and he sighed. "File your complaints for one day. I'm actually looking forward to having Christmas dinner with you and your family."

He looked at me, his radiant smile wrinkling the corners of his eyes. Our search for Bibby had gotten sidetracked by wrapping Christmas presents and banging like bunnies between beer and pizza breaks. I was achy, the feeling of being well used lingering, and it was fucking glorious.

As his house came into view, I released his hand and took a deep breath. I hoped I hadn't forgotten anything. I had insisted Marge let me make some of my mom's cornbread, and she had finally agreed. Though I didn't know his family so well, it was my version of a Christmas gift. Cody had picked me up from the motel in the morning, and we had spent three hours in the supermarket, trying to get everything I needed before they closed at noon.

We turned into the farmhouse's driveway, and my heart started pounding, not from nerves but excitement. I'd not taken part in a family gathering since getting the job at that despicable company, and I was looking forward to all the kids running around and the heaps of food. When we got out, Cody pulled me into his arms and kissed me senseless, our PDA shielded only by the open trunk. I still wasn't used to the easiness, and I nearly looked around to see if anyone was watching.

We gathered the groceries and headed for the front door, but before we could get up the porch, the screen burst open and an army of screaming kids came barreling out. They surrounded Cody, and he dropped the groceries to lift a boy up and spin him around in the air like an airplane.

"Hey!" Marge chastised from the door. "No coats, no outside."

"Where's our presents?" a little girl asked.

"Presents? Santa didn't come yet?" Cody asked, feigning shock.

They pouted out their lips and shook their heads in unison.

"Maybe he's running late. I'm sure he'll be by soon," Cody said and directed them toward the house.

As he chatted with the kids, I grabbed the discarded bags of supplies and followed. As soon as I entered the house, a loud buzz filled my ears, several different conversations along with music from the *Babes in Toyland* movie going on at once. There were a lot of people sitting around, sipping what smelled like eggnog, and I only recognized a handful.

Someone tugged my sweater hard, and warm arms engulfed me.

"I'm so happy you could make it!" Marge said against my neck. "And look at you! All decked out. You're adorable."

"Thanks," I said, blushing as I adjusted the Santa hat Cody had insisted I wear.

As Cody reconnected with his family, I made my way to the kitchen, nodding at unfamiliar faces. I set the groceries on the counter and started pulling everything out.

Elroi stuck his head in and frowned at the stuff. "What's all this?"

"Marge promised she'd let me make my mom's famous cornbread," I explained.

"Cornbread, huh? I love that stuff. What's in it?"

"I can't tell you," I teased.

"A secret?"

"Yup."

As I set everything on the counter, Cody came to join me, his arms going around my waist. "Looks good already."

"I haven't started yet."

"I wasn't talking about the food," he whispered against my ear, then quickly backed off to bang fists with his brother.

Heat filtered through me, the tease thrilling, but I forced myself to focus on what I was doing. As Cody bantered with his brothers, I directed Marge in putting everything together. Twenty minutes later, we had filled two large baking pans with the concoction. She slid them into the oven, then clapped her hands, her eyes bright. She looked every bit Mrs. Claus.

"It should be ready just in time. Sorry we were late. The store was packed." I left out the part about stealing a quickie in the motel room.

"Of course. I always do my shopping ahead of time. Looks like you're a last-minuter like Cody. Last year he spent Christmas Eve driving to the neighboring towns in search of the toy his nephew wanted. I told him not to wait until the last minute, but did he listen?"

Grinning, I shook my head. "I've done that too many years to count, but recently I've been running around trying to get to one city or another."

"Work?"

"Yeah. My job requires that I travel a lot."

119

"What exactly is it you do?" she asked, her attention completely on me.

Her question sparked regret that I had ever brought it up. I didn't want these lovely, kind people knowing I tore companies apart and displaced jobs. "Nothing I'm proud of."

"Oh."

"I always saw myself going into agriculture, but that didn't work out," I said as I dumped the dishes in the sink.

"You mean farming?"

"No. More like crop research and development. Solve the problems of growing more in shorter time frames…. Fight world hunger. That kind of stuff."

"Why didn't you?" Cody asked as he took a dirty bowl from me.

I blinked at him, not realizing he'd heard my conversation. "My dad wanted me to follow in his footsteps."

"Ah, of course," Marge said. "Well, do what you want, I say. I mean, take Cody as an example. He's a crappy rancher, literally."

"Mom," Cody hedged.

Sensing the juicy story looming, I beamed. "Tell me."

"Excuse me. I'm going to need eggnog to get me through the day," he said, but his lips were quirked up in amusement. "Thanks, Mom, for making me break my alcohol oath."

Marge smacked me with her towel playfully. "Boy, do I have a story for you. You wash, I'll dry, and I'll tell you all about his first day on the farm."

We got a good system going as I washed the dishes, then handed them off to Marge to be dried.

Her face was bright as she recounted Cody's misadventure. "We let him adjust for a few months before introducing him to the life. We started him out with something easy, having him organize the rope and retrieve tools. He was eager to do the job, a big old smile on his face. You should have seen him! He was so adorable in his little cowboy hat."

120

"Yeah, yeah," Cody said from the corner as he sipped his eggnog.

"Get to the good part," Elroi said.

"Hush," Marge hissed. "He was having so much fun running back and forth that he wasn't paying attention to where he was going and ended facedown in a big, steaming pile of cow shit."

Marge and Elroi burst out in laughter, and I smiled as Cody rolled his eyes, a lovely blush creeping up his neck.

"Tell him about the calf that butted him in the ass," Elroi pushed.

Cody face-palmed.

"Oh, I almost forgot about that. The little guy had him running around, screaming for help."

"I swear, my ass is still sore from that love tap. Who woulda thunk calves have such thick skulls?" Cody said.

As they recounted more stories of Cody's misadventures, that tightness in my stomach eased. Cody was a good sport about it, laughing along, his shy smile permanently etched on his face.

The sound of the front door slamming cut the conversation, and an eruption of cheer drew everyone out of the kitchen. I was enjoying myself, but I was thankful for the moment of peace. Turning to the counter, I occupied myself by wiping it again despite it sparkling.

Cody's hand fell on mine, and he took the washcloth from me. I turned to regard him, his eyes bright as he took a sip of eggnog. He pulled me to his lips, the kiss commanding, and I submitted, the sweetness on his lips intoxicating.

He broke away. "You okay?"

"It's nice celebrating the holidays with someone again. I'm just not used to it, I guess."

"I'm glad we could keep you company," he said softly. "Now come meet the rest of my family."

"Okay."

Cody's presence injected confidence into my system, and though he was pulled in ten different directions, I always knew he was close by. Whether a burst of laughter or a reassuring smile passed my way, I acclimated quickly. I was introduced to his cousins and helped one of his nieces color her reindeer picture. Her name was Jenny, if I remember correctly. Dinner was announced at six, and everyone flocked to the kitchen.

Our plates loaded, Cody guided me to the back porch, and the commotion was cut in half. We sat down and enjoyed our dinner together, trading smiles as we filled our bellies with ham and potatoes and green beans. I even passed Fabio some scraps.

"Damn! This is some leet cornbread, my friend," Cody praised with a full mouth.

I was unable to help the grin on my lips. "Thanks."

When we were done, Cody took our plates and disappeared into the house. He returned in a moment and handed me my coat. "You ready?"

"Yup," I said, jumping to my feet.

We rushed back to his place, both excited to play our parts. Jules was there, and Cody handed him a plate wrapped in saran.

"Tell your mom I said thanks. I would have made an appearance, but I'm not in a celebrating mood."

"Shit. He called again, didn't he?" Cody asked.

The man sighed, looking away.

"And you answered."

He shrugged. "I'm a sucker. What can I say? I was hoping some time away might change his perspective, but from his voice, nothing has. Thanks again."

With that, Jules closed his bedroom door. Cody passed me a rueful look as he made for the closet and dug out the Santa suit. He slipped into it and I moved to help him secure the beard.

"How do I look?" Cody asked.

"Not bad."

He wagged his brows. "You want to sit on Santa's lap?"

I laughed, the idea tempting. "I would feel bad making all the little boys and girls wait."

122

Cody dug out the sacks, handed one to me, and slung the other over this shoulder.

We rushed back to the house, our sacks in tow. Cody stopped me at the door. "You remember your lines?"

"Yeah. I got this."

I stepped in with the sack and made right for the front room, where I set it down. Everyone quieted, several eyes blinking at me, the kids' mouths dropping.

"I found this outside," I started. "Did anyone lose a giant sack?"

"Not me," Marge chimed in. "What about you, Dad?"

"Nope."

"Hm, I wonder where it came from."

"It's Santa's!" one of the kids cried. "Open it."

"It does look like a Santa sack, doesn't it?" I teased.

On time, Cody knocked at the front door.

"I wonder who that could be." I rushed to the door and held it open. "Uh-oh!"

Cody hobbled in, his matching sack slung over his shoulder. Gruffly, he asked, "Has anyone seen my sack?"

The house was filled with the screams of excited kids as they jumped and clapped as Cody started revealing all the gifts hiding in the sacks. He directed the kids to make one big pile while Marge started taking pictures. I resigned myself to the back of the room, not wanting to get in the way. The whole thing was lovely, everyone laughing, their expressions rivaling the luminance of the Christmas tree.

I remembered a Christmas similar to the one unfolding before me. It hadn't been when I was a kid, but a few years ago. It was the only time Brian had followed me home for the holidays because he was having a hard time with his parents. Mom had broken out champagne, and she'd gotten a little tipsy, singing karaoke. I'd laughed so hard I thought I'd bust a gut. I could feel the happiness in the air then, and I felt it now.

"Come on, everyone around the mountain of presents," Marge said. Everyone scrambled to obey, and I wondered how they'd all fit into the snapshot—heck, I was surprised everyone was in a single room at the same time.

"Aiden!" she snapped.

"What?" I asked, caught off guard.

"Which of these things is not like the other? Get in the picture. Right now!"

Heat stung my cheeks as I awkwardly moved my feet. I took my place to the side, feeling as if I were photobombing the Bannar family's celebration. Something tugged at my shirt, and I followed, Cody pulling me in next to him. Marge set the timer, then came to join us. I put on my best smiley face for the camera.

As soon as it went off, the crowd broke, people returning to their seats. The kids started plucking presents from the pile and handing them out. I returned to my little corner, not wanting to get in the way. Colorful paper flew everywhere, the sound of it ripping filling the room, along with gasps of excitement. The girl I had helped color ran up to me to show me the *Frozen* Elsa doll she had gotten. I helped her remove the packaging, and she threw her arms around me. The hug was all too brief as she rejoined her family.

"Aiden? Where are you, boy?" Marge shouted over the din. "What are you doing hiding in the corner? Come get your gift."

I was clueless as I approached her. She must have been mistaken. I couldn't fathom why there would be something for me. I no longer felt like an interloper, but I didn't think I would have been considered for presents, having only known Cody's family for a week.

I accepted a small box covered in glittery paper. I was careful opening it, not wanting to draw attention to myself. Removing the lid to a little white box, I uncovered what appeared to be an arrowhead with some sort of rune etched into it.

"Found it when I was seven," Dwayne spoke up. "It's Shoshone, and that circle on the side is an ammonite fossil. A little something to remember us by."

I ran my thumb over the tiny fossil, the bumps detailing a snail-like shell. I tried to imagine the hands that had carved the arrowhead, and the little boy who had found it years later. It was an amazing piece of history, and it invoked the same sense of wonder Bibby's letters had. But more than that, I was touched that Cody's father had gifted me one of his most prized possessions.

"Thank you," I said, my voice cracking, and I wanted to hide more than ever. I stuck the arrowhead back in the box and cradled it. My own father had never given me such a gift. His idea of Christmas presents was lectures on the importance of getting a good job.

As I watched the kids play with their new toys and Cody's family joke with one another, something broke inside me. I'd never have this again, never spend a few quiet nights with Mom and Brian, celebrating. Had I been a big boy and told her the truth, Brian might have spent last Christmas with us…. That tightness returned with a vengeance, my head swelling, my throat closing. I tried to push the thought away, but I failed.

Spending time with Cody and searching for Bibby had been a wonderful Band-Aid, but the wounds were still too fresh, every move reminding me they were there. I quietly slipped out to the back porch and into the cold night. Overhead, the stars glittered, the pale form of the mountains looming in the distance. I felt as cold and stiff as the frozen ground.

A burst of laughter spilled out from the house, and it hurt, the pain spearing me right in the heart. What the hell was I doing here? I was out of control, bouncing around in a million directions with no anchor in sight. I had no idea what I was doing or how to get back on track.

The sound of the door squeaking was an intrusion to my cold little world, and I remained still, hoping whoever was behind me would go away.

"Aiden?"

Cody's voice was both welcome and uninvited. I felt his presence immediately, his aura like a warm blanket wrapping around me. He was quiet for a long moment, the sound of his breath gentle to my ears.

"Are you okay?" he asked carefully.

I shook my head, concentrating on trying to steady myself, the tension in my head growing. I wished he would go away, walk right back into his house and celebrate with his family. It suddenly became hard to breathe, my chest tightening, the cold air soaking deep in my lungs.

Solid arms came around me, and I wanted to push him away, but I couldn't find the strength to do so. He held me tenderly, his fingers digging into my sweater, his heat thawing my limbs. I clutched the little box tightly, the weight like a rock holding me in place.

"It's okay," he whispered.

I wanted to argue, wanted to yell at him for being so good to me when I didn't deserve it. Cody was a blazing ball of light, and I was afraid to dampen it with my darkness. He whispered reassurances over and over, his warmth soothing me, his body steadying me. Something wet touched my cheek, and the ache loosened. Strange sounds fell from my lips.

"I never got the chance to tell her," I managed, surprised by the words. "I wanted to tell Mom so badly I was gay, but I didn't know how she'd take it. I wanted to… now I'll never know. And my father… I suppose on some level I'd known he didn't approve of homosexuality from a young age, and I let it influence my decision to keep myself from Mom."

I was vaguely aware I was bawling like a baby, but I was unable to hold the sobs in anymore… and I didn't want to. Cody stayed with me through every undignified choke and sniffle, his arms tight around me, his strength keeping me on my feet. I cried until my lungs hurt and my nose ran. After a long while, I managed to collect myself.

"I just wish I could go back and let her know who I really was. I wish I had gone to school for what I wanted to. I wish I could do everything all over again, but I can't, and it fucking hurts. I've been going through life numb, and I'm sick of it, but I don't know any other way. I don't know how to deal with it anymore. I wish it would just go away."

"Cody, hon? Aiden? Where are you guys?" Marge's voice rang out.

"It's okay, Mom. We're just getting some air," Cody called back, then gripped my hand. "Come with me."

I was too weak to protest, my legs moving as he pulled me toward the forest. As we passed the tree line, the sound of my shoes crunching through the snow was deafening. When the covered bridge came into view, I frowned. He led me down and underneath. The creek had frozen over, and it looked as cold and stiff as I felt.

"Right here." Cody pointed at the still ground where a log lay. "It's where I contemplated suicide for the first time in my life. I mean, I've always hated certain things about myself, but before that moment, I never thought the world might be better without me or me without it."

His declaration shocked me, and I blinked at him, his face pale in the darkness, but it was clear he was uncomfortable talking about it. He looked down to the hollowed-out log and proceeded to stare, and I knew he was reliving the moment.

"It was the day after prom. At the time I managed to laugh it off, but later... I don't know how to explain the hurt he caused. I remember thinking why couldn't I be normal like everyone else? Then we could be friends again. Despite the enormous support for my coming out, I couldn't stop thinking about those few that objected. All I could think was I'd end up disappointing Mom and Dad again and that they'd always have to hear the cruel names. I didn't want them to hurt like that. And I didn't want to get sent back."

I wanted to say something to soothe him, but my ravaged mind couldn't put anything together. He took a seat on the log, and I followed.

Cody rested his head against my shoulder. "Do you want to know what saved me?"

"Yes."

"It was Mark. He lives down the road, and bridge trail is a shortcut from his house to the main road. I can still remember the way his shoes hit the wood… like he was intruding upon a very sacred moment. I didn't know it was him at first, but I guess he heard me crying. It was late spring, so the creek was higher and I was wet and cold, and he wrapped his jersey around me. He sat right where you are now. He didn't say anything, just held me as I made a mess of myself. We'd been friends, but never particularly close until that moment."

As his words penetrated me, I concentrated on picturing this gorgeous, perpetually cheerful guy hiding under the bridge, cold and alone. It was hard to imagine such a bright soul in such a dark place. I was glad someone had been there for him, though. The world would be a lot darker without him in it.

"In that moment, I realized I was truly blessed, and that no matter if I were gay or straight, a different race or mentally ill, or a geek, there were people who loved me. Equally, there would always be people who don't approve. You can't let them get to you. I think it's why I fight so hard for equality and civil rights. Everyone deserves to be happy, but it's not a perfect world, and I hate seeing people hurt each other."

After a long moment, I mumbled, "The world is better with you in it."

"Yeah, I know. Come on. Let's go back to my place for some quiet time. It's getting cold out," he said, getting to his feet.

He offered me his hand, and I took it, his fingers entwining with mine as if our hands had been made for the purpose of connecting.

CHAPTER FOURTEEN

I WATCHED as Cody slipped out of his Santa suit, the image of his near-naked body bringing a smile to my lips. My eyes stung, but the tension in my sinuses had eased. I wasn't entirely sure why I was here, but I didn't question it. I considered any time spent with Cody to be a gift.

Placing the suit over a chair, he said, "You want me to run and get you some dessert?"

"No, I'm not hungry."

"I figured. Would you like for me to drive you back to your motel room?"

I opened my mouth, but nothing came out. I wasn't sure if he was kicking me out gently. Then again, my breakdown had interrupted Christmas for him and his family.

"I want you to stay," he said quickly. "I mean, I know you're in a shaky place right now, but if you want some alone time, it's cool."

Hiding in a dark and silent place was appealing, but I'd done that for years, and it hadn't done me any good. "I'll only go if you come with."

He looked at me, his face creased with a big smile. "It's settled, then. You can sleep here tonight. But I need to run back to the house real fast. Will you be okay for a few minutes?"

"Yeah. I'm good. Take your time. I'm sure everyone is wondering where you are."

He clicked his tongue as he pushed his legs into his jeans. "The eggnog is flowing like a river. Mom probably forgot all about us already. Relax. I'll be back soon."

He left, closing the bedroom door behind him. When I was alone, I sighed. Oddly, I felt better, the release of all those backed-up tears doing wonders. And Cody putting everything into perspective was one hell of an eye-opener. I knew I needed to stop trying to be what my father wanted and live for myself. It was easier said than done, but admitting the truth to Cody was a big step forward.

As I ran my hands up and down my thighs, Brian popped into my mind. I wondered if he had left for Europe. Maybe he was settling into his new place right this moment and sharing drinks with new acquaintances…. Maybe he was alone.

I dug out my phone and speed-dialed him. I was surprised when he picked up.

"Hey, you! I was going to call but got distracted. Merry Christmas, Aiden."

His voice brought a smile to my face. "Same. Are you in Europe?"

"No, flight leaves next week. Spending some time with the parents."

"That's good."

"Yeah, I think we've gotten to the point where we can talk to each other without worrying about saying the wrong thing and starting an argument," he said, his words ending on a sigh. "So what are you up to? Where are you spending the holidays?"

"A friend's," I said, completely honest. "Figured I'd give Dad some space to absorb everything. Not like we did the Christmas thing anyway."

"That's good. I don't want you to be alone," he said, his voice softening.

My phone beeped, letting me know I had an incoming call. "Someone is on the other line. I'll call you tomorrow, okay? Have fun."

"Same. Love you."

I clicked over, not recognizing the number, but answered anyway. "Hello?"

"Aiden? This is Darnell. We met at your mother's funeral?"

"Oh." It took me a moment to connect the name to his face, and when I did, I thought it was strange he was calling. "I guess

I have paperwork to take care of. I assume your company is still interested in carrying on the contract with me?"

"Yes. I mean, no, that's not why I'm calling. I've gotten word you were missing and wanted to make sure everything was okay."

I chuckled because I'd nearly forgotten about Dad and Missy and my sudden absence. "No, just needed some space."

"I see. Well, I didn't mean to disturb your holiday. Merry Christmas."

"Same."

When I hung up, I realized I had no idea how he'd gotten my number or how he would know I was missing. Unless Mom had shared it with him in case he couldn't get in contact with her? Shrugging, I pushed my phone back in my pocket. I knew I had to get in contact with my family and at least let them know I was alive. I decided to fire a text off to Dad and Missy informing them I was safe and whole but not in town.

A noise in the other room drew my attention, and I cracked the door to see Cody's roommate moving laundry around. He looked as haggard as I felt, his face drawn tight, his eyes rimmed red. He noticed me, and I blanched, embarrassed at having been caught staring.

"Hi," he said. "Sorry if I disturbed you. Doing stuff keeps my mind off other things."

"No, it's okay. I mean, you live here. Happy… holidays, I guess."

He sputtered a laugh that was devoid of amusement. "Holidays, sure. Happy is debatable. Sorry, guess I'm being a Scrooge."

I stepped out of the room. "No, it's okay. I don't feel much like celebrating either. Have you been here long?"

"Almost a year. Christ… it doesn't seem like that long," he said. "It was kind of my New Year's resolution."

I nodded, intending to ask what he had resolved. I knew I had a few of my own to make. Following through was another story, but I guess it was like that for everyone.

He stopped in front of his room, and his lip went between his teeth as he ran his eyes over my body. "Be good to him, okay? He deserves it."

Before I could respond, Jules disappeared into his room.

Shrugging, I retreated back into Cody's bedroom. Jules's words followed me. Despite having a blast with Cody, I was afraid of making him sad when I left. But he had to know I would be leaving eventually. Pinching the bridge of my nose, I realized I had a lot of crap to sort through. I could safely say there was as much stuff in my head as Mom's house.

I shed my clothes and got under the covers, then waited for Cody to return. I was in a weird mood and just wanted to be close to him, even if it meant snuggling. Luckily, he returned quickly. The moment he spotted my state of undress, he stilled, his eyes hooding. A crooked smile arched over his lips.

"Best present ever." He grinned.

I lowered my eyes to the wrapped box he had in his hands. "What's that?"

A lovely blush colored his cheeks as he held it out for me. "Your Christmas present. I forgot to stick it in the sack because I'd hidden it in the garage."

I frowned, dubious, and accepted it. I looked to him for explanation, but he simply nodded. Sitting up, I tore the wrapping away. I smiled until my cheeks hurt as I ran my eyes all over the box displaying colorful pictures of bugs and body parts.

"Got it on eBay. I had it rushed overnight."

"Cody, that must have cost a fortune. You shouldn't have done that."

"Yeah, I should have." He winked, then rubbed his hands together. "Come on. Let's crack this baby open and make yucky things to eat."

He joined me on the bed as I tore it open and set everything up on the bedside table. It took a little brainpower, but we managed to figure it out. We made spiders and creepy-crawly things, Cody jiggling a centipede in front of me before devouring it.

"Not bad. A little crunchy," he teased.

"I've heard bugs are good for protein."

He licked his lips. "You know what else is good for protein?"

I laughed, but before I could jab back, he covered my lips, and I tasted sweetness. I relaxed against the bed as we kissed passionately, his hand dipping down my body. When he grabbed my cock, I hissed.

He pulled away. "Do you want to? I mean, if you're not in the mood—"

I cut off his words by pulling him back to my mouth. It didn't take me long to get hard, his skilled touches like magic.

"Tonight, it's my turn," he whispered against my jaw.

I skimmed my eyes all over his face, and he seemed like a vivid dream. A few weeks ago my life had hit a brick wall, and for the first time since Mom's death, I felt hopeful. Like things would be okay and that I wasn't as alone as I thought. I watched as he kissed his way down my body, flicking his tongue across my nipples. He pushed the blankets away to reveal my erection and settled himself between my legs. As he covered my dick with his mouth, I bowed off the bed. I closed my eyes against the assault, committing to memory the feeling of his hot, wet mouth around my cock.

He slunk back up my body to straddle me, my dick sandwiched between his asscheeks. I held him close, his smooth, hot skin warming me to my core. I felt like the winter ground awaking to the spring warmth. He reached into the bedside table and produced a condom and some lube. I watched, fascinated, as he rolled the condom down my cock, then slicked his ass. He was all smiles as he sat down on me, the hot tightness of his ass wonderfully shocking.

His head tipped back in pleasure, and I gripped his hips as he screwed me slow and deep, every motion heaven. It wasn't long before we were both panting and grunting. I bucked upward, the pleasure surging forward.

Leaning close, he pushed me down. "Relax, Speedy."

I growled but accepted. He seemed entirely pleased with himself, his lips claiming mine. The way his tongue stroked mine stole most of my protests, and I pulled him close, keeping him tight against my body. I thrust upward, the motion slow and careful, and he moaned. Invigorated, I flipped him over and repeated the thrust, his gasp injecting confidence into my system. I focused on him and his reactions, letting him guide me.

As my climax grew closer, it was hard to keep from pounding into him. When he clawed my ass, I thrust deep. The crude words spilling from his lips were like an accelerant, and I fucked him faster… harder. Cody came first, and I followed right behind, our voices echoing through the room until I could move no more.

I collapsed back on the bed. "Oh, I so needed that."

Cody chuckled. "You and me both."

He got up and slid the condom off me, then disappeared out the door. He was back a moment latter, giggling like a girl. He tossed me a towel, and I cleaned myself off.

"Jules almost caught me running around bare-assed naked. I forgot he was here."

He returned to bed, and I pulled him close to me, his arms going around me, and I didn't know how I'd ever cope without having him near. I knew I couldn't stay here forever, but for now I wanted nothing more than to be close to this blinding ball of light.

"Hey, you okay?" he asked.

"Yeah. This is shaping up to be one of the best Christmases ever," I mumbled against his shoulder. "Thank you for sharing it with me."

"Are you kidding? The more the merrier."

CHAPTER FIFTEEN

THE MOMENT the motel door closed, Cody claimed my lips, and I didn't mind one bit.

"Jack Frost has been nipping at my lips, and I needed something to warm them," he teased.

"You need anything else warmed?" I poked back.

He laughed. "I'll take you up on that later."

I nodded, and we shed our winter clothes. It had started snowing in the morning, the fat flakes piling up to a healthy five inches. I couldn't describe the feeling the snow-covered pines invoked in me. It was so beautiful I wanted to cry.

Cody dug out my uncle's footlocker and set it on the bed. I was glad he was taking the initiative, because I was content with dallying with him. I had to remind myself why I'd come here and that I still had responsibilities back home. But I wasn't going anywhere until we found Bibby or verified he was dead. We had both agreed that we needed to look through all the letters for any possible clues—names, locations, anything that might aid us in our search. And now Christmas was over, we had no excuse not to get shit done.

We went through the letters, Cody reading out loud and tearing up every now and then. I teased him about going broke on tissue paper, and he pushed me playfully. The day went on around us as we read, the sound of people laughing outside, wheels spinning in the snow, the sky slowly darkening. As we neared the end of the stash, the correspondence grew darker, Bibby wanting to know why Georgie was pushing him away. The waterworks was turned on full, and even I shed a tear as Bibby laid his heart and soul on paper, begging Georgie not to leave him.

"That's it?" Cody asked as he searched the chest. "No way. I need to know what happened."

He looked devastated as he frantically organized the letters.

I pulled out the little box that held my uncle's Medal of Honor. "Georgie died overseas."

Taking the box, Cody shook his head in denial but said nothing as he ran his fingers over the medal. A tense silence courted us as he fiddled with the box, the frustration evident on his face. The idea of never knowing what had happened filled my head with tears, but I held them back. I didn't want to fall apart again. Once was enough.

His gasp drew my attention, and I realized he had accidently popped the velvet backing out.

"Sorry, I didn't mean to—" His words cut off, and his brows went down as he slowly peeled it away to reveal an envelope. "It's still sealed. And it's from your uncle." Cody carefully peeled it open and withdrew the folded piece of paper. "It's dated February 16, 1960."

"That's the day he died," I said, agape.

With a deep breath, he started reading.

My Dearest Bibby,

By the time you receive this letter, I will be on a ship. It will take weeks to reach America, and I know it will feel like years for both of us. The sea is such a vast thing that sometimes I think it is a path unto infinity, a place where war has no meaning and things are far removed from petty ideals. I've seen the ocean so many times, but never before have I looked at it with such hope and resolve. The war has taught me many harsh lessons, but I am thankful for one. It has shown me that life is fragile and should be cherished.

I survived. As I rode the train, I was afraid I'd never see you again. When a gun was shoved into my hands, I was terrified of having to kill someone. As I watched my friends fall beside me, I resigned myself to death. But I made it. You were with me every step of the way. It was your voice I heard, your face I saw, your heat that kept me warm on cold nights, and when I thought I couldn't go on, your blood flowed through me.

I was a fool to have thrown that away. I suppose the war should have hardened me, but I am still afraid. I worry what my mother will say about us, and I can't bear to hear the cruel words that will undoubtedly be thrown at you. But the world is a cruel place, and we make it that way. If we are lucky, we don't have to endure that cruelty alone.

I love you. I love you more than I can describe. There are no flowery words that can detail what I feel for you. There is no one who can tell me my love is misplaced or immoral. I know I hurt you, but I don't want to live in fear. I want to be free. I want to be happy. I want to love you for as long as I live and be loved by you.

If you can find it in your heart to forgive me, then meet me at the docks. The voyage will be maddening, the slow drip of time frustrating, but I choose you, my love. I will tell you so in front of everyone. I will cry it to the sky.

Please, wait for me.

Forever Yours,
Georgie

Cody looked at me with glassy eyes, his voice hardly more than a whisper. "Oh my God, Aiden. Do you know what this means? Georgie chose Bibby in the end. But he never got a chance to send it. If Bibby is alive, we have to find him! He needs to know."

I nodded but didn't allow myself to get too excited. Happy endings were too rare to expect, but I didn't want to dash his hopes. He practically flew out of his seat and landed on top of me, kissing me senseless. He gasped and backed away, cradling the letter against his chest as if it were precious. Carefully, he slid it back into the envelope.

"We have to find him," he said again, his voice cracking. He started toward me but froze. "Wait. If Georgie died in the war, why was he on his way to a ship to take him home?"

I frowned. "My mother said he died in the war the few times she mentioned him."

"But she didn't specifically say he died in action? If he had been discharged and was preparing to go back home, then how did he die? Aiden... this doesn't make any sense."

I bit the inside of my cheek, then glanced at the paperwork I'd found inside the medal box. I unfolded some documents and read carefully but came up empty. "There's no death certificate or anything that states the cause of death."

"The Army would have sent his belongings back to his family. I'm betting the letter was on his person when he was killed. But it doesn't make any sense. He was on his way home... he shouldn't be dead. It's—"

"Heartbreaking," I finished for him.

As we looked at each other, the implications hit us, and the pressure in my head swelled. I didn't bother hiding it. It was a damned tragedy that these two people who had loved each other so deeply had been separated after going through so much. Georgie should have made it home. They should have shared a wonderful life together.

"We still need to find Alice. Maybe she knows what really happened? Wait, are your grandparents alive?"

"No, most of my family on Georgie's side is long gone. Besides, I don't really talk to my family much. Mom was all I had."

He looked away sullenly, his expression reflecting pure sorrow. I wondered what it was like to feel as deeply as he did, and

I wasn't sure if it was a curse or a gift. But Cody inspired me to be a better person. If I could accomplish one tenth of what he had, I'd die a happy man.

"As a living heir, you can request a copy of the death certificate," he said, ruffling his hair.

"Come here," I commanded, and he obeyed. I pulled him close and buried my face in the crook of his neck, his arms holding me tightly. The letters had left us in a state of heightened emotion, and I knew he needed a little cuddle time as much as I did.

"Are we still on for tomorrow?" he asked after a while.

I craned my head so I could see his gorgeous face. "Tomorrow?"

"The fundraiser."

"I forgot about that. Yeah, I will go with you," I said, running my fingers down his cheek. I still couldn't grasp that I was in Montana, spending my nights with this amazing man. It seemed like a fairy tale, but I knew there wasn't a happy ending to this little adventure.

"Good, because it will be fun, and you could use fun."

I chuckled. "No kidding."

"HEY, GORGEOUS," Cody said as he walked into my motel room the next afternoon. "You ready?"

I blinked at him, my phone still in my hand.

Frowning, he asked, "What's wrong?"

"I just got fired," I said blankly. I was sure it hadn't quite sunk in yet.

"Shit. I'm sorry."

His expression read all tenderness, but I burst out in gut-splitting laughter. When I came down, he was watching me carefully, concern crossing his face. I took a few deep breaths, then started explaining. "It was a shit job, anyway. I lied about what I do… did. When I applied, I thought I would be helping ailing companies, but I what I really do is take them over and sell them off for profit piece by piece. You don't know how many people lost their jobs because of me."

He came to sit next to me, his presence welcome, but I couldn't look him in the eye. I was afraid of disappointing him. I wasn't sure why I needed his approval so badly.

"My first job was at a coat factory. A part-time thing to make a little extra cash. Anyway, they had a massive inventory of real fur. I felt like I'd betrayed my furry friends for working there. I mean, I'm all for hunting—everything is used, you know? Meat, skin, bone. But to kill a living creature for vanity? I... sorry, I'm rambling again."

"How do you do that?"

He looked at me quizzically. "Do what?"

"No matter how bad things seem, you say just the right words to make me feel better."

He grinned, his eyes sparkling. "I'm good like that, baby."

Chuckling, I shook my head in disbelief.

"What will you do now?" Cody inquired, punching my thigh.

"I have no idea. I never wanted to go into business, but I thought it would make my father happy. I should have known better. He never even attended my graduation. Maybe it's for the best. It made me miserable."

He took my head between his palms and planted a big kiss on my lips. "There's your answer. You need to find what makes you happy, Aiden. Going through life miserable is no way to live. Me, I love doing what I do. Meeting new people, connecting with them, and seeing the world when I can. I don't think I could do anything else. If I were dirt poor, I'd still be happy."

As he went on, I committed everything about him to memory—the way his lips pulled up, the sound of his voice, the way he used his hands to accentuate a point. Cody was my idol, the person I looked up to and aspired to be. He made me feel confident about my situation, as if I could weather my disapproving family and stand strong against the cruel words that would no doubt be thrown my way. I thought I might be falling for him. Terrified, I pushed that thought to the back of my brain.

"What is the highlight of your life?" I asked quickly, interrupting him. "Of all the things you've done and the places you've seen, what is your favorite?"

"When I went down to Joplin, Missouri, to help with the relief effort. Mark, DeShawn, Jarome, and I collected food and clothes, then drove down there. It was devastating seeing all those houses reduced to toothpicks... the people. Jesus. Helping people... I can't describe what it feels like. I pretty much walked around in a perpetual state of shock. At that moment, I felt as if my life had true meaning. There was a time when I thought I was a failure. I mean, what can one person do? But the experience solidified my resolve to do whatever I can. All we have is one another in this world."

"You're like fucking Yoda, I swear," I said, blown away by his unfailing kindness.

"But cuter, right?" Taking a much-needed breath, he stood up and held his hand out. "Come on. Let's go have some fun."

I smiled until my cheeks ached, his fingers entwining with mine. I never wanted to let go, but I knew I couldn't stay. I realized it was going to hurt like a motherfucker when I left.

The party was already going by the time we arrived, and Cody navigated us through the crowd slowly, stopping every two seconds to greet people and introduce me. All the attention was a little unnerving, but Cody stayed close, passing me smiles of reassurance. We handed over our fifty-dollar entry fee and accepted the wristbands, then headed over to the buffet.

As Cody fetched two plates, I leaned in and inquired, "Who is this for, anyway?"

"I'm so sorry! I guess I should have told you. Pete Moss, the best damned politician ever to sit in Montana office. He's a local boy too. He helped push the bill for marriage equality to the Senate and is working to get money out of politics. He always seems to find time to listen to me ramble about one thing or another. A true American hero. He found out he has cancer a few months ago."

We loaded our plates with all kinds of fried food as he went on talking about all the meetings he had with the man. Most of the tables were taken, so we took a seat at the bar and chowed down.

"Hey, don't lose your tickets. They're for the raffle. You could win a basket with lots of nice-smelling soap."

Shoving the tickets in my pocket, I asked, "Is this the fundraiser Wylie was organizing?"

"Yeah. I wonder where he is. I haven't seen him yet. He's probably busy with something or other. Events like these are labor intensive. I was hoping he might give us one of his charity dances, but I guess he is swamped. He taught me a few moves."

As the evening went on, the music played, and so many people came to greet Cody, I'd lost count. Gigi stopped by, along with DeShawn and Jarome. Mark eventually arrived with a girl, his face bright as he banged fists with me. Even Marge and Dwayne made an appearance. I wondered what it was like to have so many friends and people who cared about you. I'd never seen such warmth. I resigned myself to watching Cody interact with them, his charisma infectious as they laughed.

The night flew by, the hours bleeding into one another, and though I mostly kept to myself, I enjoyed being a part of something so important. When the band cut off and announced it was time for karaoke, Cody gasped and dashed for the stage, leaving me in a cloud of dust.

"This is going to be good," Mark teased, leaning against the bar.

I grinned, my insides bouncing at the prospects of hearing Cody sing.

"Thanks, everyone, for coming. I'm Cody," he said as he accepted the microphone.

"No shit," someone shouted.

He winked at them. "Hiram Parker, all the way in the back there. You know him. Let's give him some hands. He's pledged five hundred bucks for everyone that gets up here and sings."

The crowd cheered, and the guy tipped his head.

"Like I was saying. This was my idea, so I was told I have to go first." Everyone clapped, and he signaled the DJ. When the song popped up on the screen, he face-palmed, and a wave of laughter filtered through the crowd. He turned to the DJ and made a rude gesture. "You did that on purpose because you knew I was going first."

"Rick roll, rick roll," people started chanting.

"Okay, okay. Let's get this done."

As the music began, my cheeks started to hurt again. Cody was an amazing guy, but he was a horrible singer. As he went through the song out of sync, the room burst out in amused cheers, but he barreled on. I couldn't help joining in. When it ended, Cody moseyed over to the DJ and whispered something in his ear. He returned to the center of the stage.

"You know what my mom told me in first grade? 'Babe, I love you, but you can't sing.' You know what she told me in second grade? 'Boy, you can't sing, but you got moves.'"

Cody handed the mic off to someone as the music burst over the speakers, Fatboy Slim's "The Rockafeller Skank" filling the room.

"Oh my God, he's not," I heard Mark mumble.

Cody might be a horrible singer, but he was a smooth dancer, every move in tune with the hard beat, his body flowing like liquid. I joined in the cheers as he busted one move after another, and laughed when he threw in a classic crotch grab. People started to join him on the stage, and when he pointed at me, I shook my head, but my legs started moving. Before I knew it, I was dancing with him on stage, whatever reservations I might have had floating away. By the time the song ended, I was huffing and puffing, sweat gracing my brow.

Before I knew it, midnight had rolled in, and one of the staff announced they had raised over twenty grand. I didn't end up winning any of the raffles, but I felt like a million bucks.

As we walked back to my Hummer, Cody wrapped his arm around my shoulders and pulled me close.

"You had fun," he said.

"I did. I had no idea you could dance like that."

He chuckled. "Dirty dancing. It's Mom's favorite movie, and I was so in love with Patrick Swayze that I would practice his dance moves in front of the mirror."

I wagged my brows. "The Lover Boy scene was pretty hot."

"I know, right?" He gasped and stopped in his tracks. "You distracted me! I forgot to tell you my great-uncle Rob is coming home from Hawaii in a few days. Mom told me he knew some people that lived in the Garden. Maybe he can help us."

I knew I should be more excited, but the closer we got to solving the mystery of Bibby, the sooner it would come time for me to leave. I wasn't ready to let this fantasy go.

"So. The night is young. We are young. What would you like to do?" Cody inquired.

I looked to the sky and teased playfully, "I'm sure we can think of a few things."

He snickered, the expression he gave me letting me know he was on board with the plan. We didn't say anything else, the easy silence between us comfortable. When we got to my car, he surprised me by pressing me against the door and claiming my lips. The parking lot was full of people returning to their vehicles, and my first instinct was to see if anyone was watching. But Cody commanded my full attention, and I succumbed to him, opening completely.

He withdrew, his eyes hooded as he licked his lips. "Motel?"

I grinned and pulled him back to me by the collar of his coat. When our cocks met through our pants, we groaned against each other's lips. "Okay, yeah."

As Cody ran around to the driver's side, I realized the parking lot was empty. Christ, that boy had a way of making me crazy.

When we got back to the motel room, my phone chimed again to let me know I had another missed call. I had hoped it was Brian, but as my father's number flashed across the screen, I sighed miserably. I knew I couldn't ignore him or Missy forever, but I wasn't going to let them ruin the moment.

Cody came up from behind me, his arms solid, and I felt safe in his embrace. He kissed my neck, his fingers dipping under my shirt. His voice was a purr against my ear. "You think I got some leet dance moves? You haven't seen anything yet."

I grinned as he pushed me down onto the bed. I had no doubt he was going to rock my world.

CHAPTER SIXTEEN

"SOMETHING IS bothering you. I can tell," Cody said as he drove us to his Uncle Rob's house the next day.

"My father called again this morning," I said on a sigh.

"Let me guess. He's the ringleader of that group that doesn't agree with your choices?"

I nodded, watching the snow-covered trees pass. I had cracked the window, and the crisp, cool air flying in helped in leveling my mood. "The day after Mom's funeral, my ex came over. My father walked in on us fooling around. Needless to say, he wasn't very happy. Went on about me needing help and how he was glad Mom didn't know before she died."

"I'm sorry. That's a terrible thing to say. I don't understand how the people closest to us can be the cruelest." He took my hand, and I accepted it, glad for the simple comfort.

"I know I can't run from him forever, but I don't need that right now. Mourning for my mother is hard enough without trying to explain to him why I'm gay. I don't get why he's so concerned with my life, considering he hasn't been in it for nearly twenty years. I guess I'm bitter that he just didn't leave Mom, but me as well."

"I know what that is like." When I eyed him, he explained, "My birthparents were both alcoholics and druggies. That's how I got taken away. They never came to claim me, missed all the court-appointed visitations. I can't describe the feeling something like that invokes. I was lucky, though, with Mom and Dad adopting me."

His pain came through his voice, and I wanted to snuggle him. I hated that he knew what it felt like to be alone. Though I knew Mom had loved me, I sorely missed my father. "I'm glad you have people who love you."

He looked at me, and his lip went between his teeth for an instant. "You do too. Your mother. Just because she is gone doesn't mean her love is. And Fabio. He loves you bunches."

I chuckled, amazed how he could make me smile so easily. "I'm sure my breakfast had something to do with it. So your uncle…. You really think he can help us?" I inquired, needing to change the subject.

"I don't know, but it is worth trying. Maybe he can lead us in the direction of Alice. That would be a huge breakthrough. But I haven't seen him in forever, and I miss him."

The rest of the drive was silent, fat flakes drifting in the air. I watched the trees pass, and when they broke, I gazed up to the mountains that seemed to touch heaven. I wished Mom could have seen this place. I had resolved to make contact with my father soon. I would be adamant about who I was, and if he couldn't accept it, that was his problem. Same would go for Missy. For a brief moment, I considered following Brian to Europe. Who knew, a change in continent might do me wonders.

"Here it is," Cody announced as we turned into a gated community.

"Uncle Rob is ancient, but don't tell him that. He has the enthusiasm of a five-year-old. His knees are another story, though," Cody said, his amusement lighting up his face.

"He travels a lot?"

"Oh, yeah. He's been all over. Says we only live once, and we are supposed to enjoy it while we can. I don't see him very often, but he is kind of a personal hero to me," Cody said. "If I'm lucky, he brought me souvenirs."

I pictured Cody in a Hawaiian shirt and nothing else, his glorious form against a setting sun. I'd never fucked on a beach, and the idea was arousing. I swore I'd never get enough of him. The daydream was lovely, but I returned to reality as Cody pulled his car into a driveway. I stretched, the ride seeming longer than it had been.

"Kid, that you?" A voice rang out, and I spotted an elderly man dressed in khakis and a colorful shirt peering through a screen.

"You better believe it!" Cody shouted as he raced for the door like a kid barreling for a toy store.

I managed to keep up and grinned at the sight of Cody snuggling his uncle, the man tiny compared to Cody.

"Christ, y-y-you like a dog, jumpin' on me!" Uncle Rob chortled, his cheeks rising. He reminded me of Santa Claus on vacation, his cheeks flushed from excitement, his fuzzy beard like snow.

"I missed you!"

"Yeah, yeah—hey, who is your friend?" the man asked as he pushed his glasses up his nose.

Cody gasped in delight. "This is my friend Aiden, all the way from Texas. I'm helping him find someone. Aiden, this is my favorite uncle, Rob."

I waved shyly.

"Texas, huh? Can't imagine why you'd want to be from there," Rob said as he hobbled toward me. His strong handshake was like a quake vibrating through me, but I smiled. "Come on in."

We all filed into the house, and I was taken aback by the familiarity. Knickknacks lined shelves, and mementos from various places lay scattered on tables. The guy must have seen every corner of the world.

"Did you bring me anything back from Hawaii, Unc?" Cody inquired, his expression hopeful.

The man made a sound of disbelief. "Of course I did. Hey! What's the first thing a Hawaiian girl does when she wakes up in the morning? She goes home!"

Cody winked suggestively at his uncle. "Speaking from experience?"

"Ha! Not me!"

"Suuuuurrrre...."

"Okay, kid. Want to play dirty?"

"I surrender!" Cody chuckled. "Seriously... where's my presents?"

I plopped my ass on the couch and nearly sank right through as Cody sat next to me. Rob retrieved a big duffle bag and set it on the coffee table.

"Let's see... oh, here we go," Rob said as he pulled out some strings of flower garlands and set them around our necks. "And they are the pl-pl-plastic ones, so they will last forever."

When he handed Cody a dancing hula girl, Cody frowned. "You can get this anywhere."

"Nuh... this one is special. It's made in Hawaii."

Beaming, Cody flipped it over and showed me the "Made in Taiwan" stamp.

"Oh, what about this? I saw it and thought of you!"

Cody caught the package, a blush creeping up his neck. "Really, Unc? I didn't know they had a Spencer's Gifts in Hawaii."

I stifled my laugh as I imagined Cody in the elephant underwear, his cock nestled in the trunk. I'd known Uncle Rob for all of five minutes, and I could see the man was the source of Cody's sense of humor... and I liked him for that reason alone.

"Here's something I thought was really awesome," he said, producing a shiny black rock. "It's volcanic glass, I'm told right out of Kilauea. Be careful. It's heavy."

Making a sound of delight, Cody accepted it. His fingers traced the grooves. Turning to me, he dumped it in my palms. "Check this out."

The volcanic glass was pretty cool, and I pictured it being dug out from the side of a mountain.

The man sat down in a La-Z-Boy and sighed. "I'm getting old."

"You've been getting old for the last ten years," Cody said. "And you're still going. What's next? Where are you headed?"

Stroking his chin, Rob looked at the ceiling. "I was thinking Florida."

"What!" Cody shrieked. "Tell me you're not retiring!"

"No way, kid. I would need to have a job first. My old bones just need to thaw. B-b-besides…. Florida has all the hotties, don't you know?"

"I wish I did."

"You want to come with, kid? Just us two. Oh, that would be so much fun! I heard they be having that White Party there for you. Oh, and the cocktails. Florida has good cocktails, right?"

Cody mashed his fist into his cheek. "That would be awesome, but I have a lot going on here right now. With my blog and helping Jules and Aiden."

"Don't let me stop you," I chimed in. They craned their heads toward me, and I felt as if I'd intruded upon a sacred moment. I managed to sink a little farther into the couch.

Cody gasped, as if remembering why we were here. "Uncle Rob, you said you knew people that lived in the Garden."

"What about it?" he asked, his tone dropping.

"Well, Aiden came all the way from Texas to…." He looked at me, and I shrugged, figuring we might as well be upfront about everything. "He is looking for someone. You see, he found these old love letters in his mom's attic from the fifties. They're amazing…. Anyway, we're having a hard time finding the guy who wrote them… Bibby. We are positive it's an alias, and they were probably sent to a friend's because… ah, well. They were two guys, and back then, it wasn't accepted." He took a deep breath, then turned to me. "I'm not making any sense, am I? Can we show him?"

"Sure," I said, figuring it was pointless to hide them anymore.

Cody was out of his seat and through the door as if he had strapped a rocket to his ass. I shook my head, his enthusiasm getting my pumper going. I turned to ask Rob if he knew Alice but stopped. His cheery expression was gone, and his eyes seemed glued to the floor. Cody was back in an instant, the footlocker snug in his hands. He sat next to me and started going on about the letters, completely unaware of his uncle's reaction.

I nudged Cody, and he blinked at me. He must have sensed the tension because he watched Rob for a long moment. "Uncle? What's wrong?"

The man looked between us before his gaze settled on the case. "Would you like some tea? I bought some of this bubble stuff. Don't ask me why they call it that. It's supposed to b-b-be really good."

"Okay," Cody said, then offered me a shrug.

As Rob moved around in the kitchen, his attention was constantly drawn to us. "That a military box, isn't it?"

"Yeah," I spoke up. "It was my great-uncle George's, but I never met him."

The sound of a cup shattering on the floor sent Cody to his feet, and he rushed into the kitchen.

"Duh-duh-duh!" the man sputtered. "I can do it, ki-ki-kid!"

"Are you sure you're okay?" Cody asked dubiously. "You never stutter this bad unless—"

"Go sit with your friend. I'll b-b-be right there," he ordered, waving Cody away.

Cody returned, his expression pensive. I suddenly felt out of place but didn't know what to do other than remain quiet and still. Cody chewed his lip as Rob made the tea, and I was of a mind to suggest we come back later, but I really wanted to find the treasure. I felt as if Cody's uncle was our last chance.

"You never met your uncle?" Rob asked as he poured some tea into shot glasses. "Your mother knew him?"

"I don't think so. Not well, anyway. She told me she was just a baby when he died," I said and accepted the glass, doing my best to be polite.

Cody sipped at the glass as Rob returned to his seat. "Hey, this isn't too bad."

Rob sampled his own, then made a face and set it on the table. "Well, I was never one for tea. Coffee is more my thing. Hell, give me a bottle of brandy and I'm happy. Better yet… coffee and brandy."

"What about coffee and tea? Like the bacon-and-chocolate thing?"

"What kind of harebrained idea is that?" Rob chided and turned to me. "Is Audrey with you?"

The question speared me, but I collected myself quickly. "No, she passed away recently."

He nodded, that distant look shining in his eyes again. Speaking about her didn't hurt quite as much as I thought it would.

"I should say I'm sorry, shouldn't I? I never understood that part," Rob said. "Can I ask how?"

Taking a deep breath to steady myself, I had to force the words out. "Car accident."

He nodded, looking down, his eyes glassy. Cody gave me a reassuring touch, his palm smooth and warm against my arm. I could feel his excitement and didn't fault him for brushing the issue of my mother's death aside.

Cody sat forward, his tone laced with suspicion. "Uncle, did you know someone named Bibby that lived in the Garden?"

"Jeebus, but it's been ages since I heard that name."

Cody grabbed my arm, his grip crushing my bones. I nearly clawed at his thigh in response as I leaned closer, my curiosity piqued.

"You know him? You have to tell us!" Cody demanded.

Rob looked at Cody. "I kinda do."

Cody pumped his fist in the air, then shook me until I vibrated with laughter. Shooting to his feet, Cody started detailing our search and every dead end. I couldn't help smiling as I watched him animate our journey. A huge part of me couldn't believe this was real. I was sure I'd heard wrong.

"Kid, you're going to make me dizzy."

"Wait," I said. "Are you sure? I mean, he went to great lengths *not* to be found—"

"Are you the friend? Tell me he had the letters sent to you! Oh my God! This is awesome! Can we break out the champagne? Come on, Unc, this is the special occasion you were talking about."

Rob looked at him bashfully. "I drank it."

"What! You said we'd share it one day." At that, he slumped down next to me. "Really, Uncle Rob? What was he like? You have to tell us."

"Never mind that," I cut in. "Is he still alive?"

Cody smacked himself in the forehead. "Yeah, is he?"

"Well… that's a good question. Let me ask you something, Aiden. What be your interest? Why you come all the way from Texas to find him?"

I opened my mouth, but nothing came out. I wanted to tell him, I really did, but I was afraid to risk embarrassment for my brash actions. But Cody hadn't thought I was silly. Maybe Rob wouldn't either.

"What does it matter?" Cody asked.

"Is matters to me," Rob replied.

"I needed to do something," I spoke up, surprised by my own words. "I was… am at a weird place in my life, and I needed to do something for me. I wanted to meet this guy because… I just needed to do something for me."

The moment the words passed my lips, heat fluttered through me, my heart pounding in my ears. It wasn't so much embarrassment as finally having an answer to what I was doing out here. Everything I'd done in my life had been to make my father proud, but I had come to realize it had made me miserable in the process.

"Well… we all got to do what we got to do, I reckon," Rob said, stroking his chin.

After a long moment, Cody burst out, "Oh come on, you two! You're killing me. I *need* to know."

"Hold your horses, kid. Don't rush me. You know I don't like bein' rushed."

"I can't help it."

Rob pursed his lips, apparently deep in thought. I figured he'd gotten used to hiding Bibby and was reluctant to reveal the man's location. Did that mean he was still alive? Possibility bloomed before me—I might actually meet Bibby.

"We need to give him something," I blurted, then pulled out the letter from the medal case. "We found it a few days ago. It was sealed, and… we were hoping to give it to him. He should know."

I watched as Rob's hand connected with the envelope, his fingers grazing mine for an instant. He ran his thumb along the corners. After a long moment he finally said, "Kid, can you get my suitcase? You know, the one I hide all my money in."

Cody shot to his feet and raced through the house. He returned in an instant with an old leather suitcase. He plopped next to me, and we watched pensively as Rob undid the clasps and lifted the lid. He set several stack of papers aside, along with a Ziploc bag of cash.

He pulled out an old photo and handed it to Cody. I leaned in, running my eyes over the black-and-white snapshot of two men standing side by side against some trees, their faces creased with smiles, their arms wrapped around each other's waists.

Agape, I said, "That one is my uncle George."

"Yep."

"Is this Bibby?" Cody asked, his brow creased.

"It was," Rob confirmed. "But that was a long time ago, and time has a way of changing us. Sometimes for the worse, but often for the better."

I cleared my throat, feeling as if I was slipping between dimensions, my body leaving Rob's couch. A few days ago I had resolved myself to the possibility of never finding Bibby, but the whole thing was like a carrot on a stick, and I realized my need to know had to do with me rather than him. I wanted to leave my miserable life behind, become something new and shiny and happy. I wanted to live a life worth living and have something to show for my time on this earth.

Audrey.

Rob's words bounced around in my brain. In time, I knew I would get past the grief of losing Mom and learn to deal with having hid myself from her. Maybe one day Dad and Missy would come to accept me as Brian's parents had done. In time, I hoped to accept the choices I'd made.

"Uncle?" Cody prompted.

Audrey.

My eyes found Rob's, his hazel orbs tracking me carefully, his fingers caressing the envelope. I waited for him to reveal Bibby's location and identity, but the seconds stretched. I had no idea what happened, everything crashing into me and knocking me senseless. I looked between the photo and Rob, my brain firing off. The rounded face, the bright eyes... my head spun, and I thought I'd pass out. Things were moving too fast, and I wasn't prepared for the brick wall rushing for me.

Audrey... how had he known Mom's name? I frantically racked my brain, trying to remember if I'd said her name, but I was sure I hadn't.

"Holy. Shit," I rasped.

"What?" Cody demanded as he looked between Rob and me. "Tell me!"

I shook my head, not entirely sure what I was saying no to. The whole thing seemed like a dream, and though I wanted to shout it out loud, I was afraid to break the possibility. What if I was wrong? What if I was so desperate I was seeing things that weren't really there? This wasn't possible; it couldn't be this easy. Luck wasn't so generous.

"Seriously, what am I missing?" Cody whimpered.

Taking a deep breath, Rob smiled. "I could hardly speak back then, you know. I just couldn't get anything out, not even my name. We met when we were eight. I was rounding the corner on my bike and slammed right into him. I tried to apologize, sure he would b-b-beat me up... all the kids did. But he held out his hand and helped me to my feet. From that point on, we were never separated. We would write cheesy poetry and read it out loud to help with my stutter. We did everything together... at least until the war. We intended to enlist together, but I failed the test. My speech was a little better then, but nowhere near their specifications. One of my legs is shorter than the other, and that didn't help either."

Cody rubbed his temples, his voice shaky, and I was sure everything was falling together for him. "My brain hurts."

I shushed him and nodded for Rob to continue.

"I never told anyone about Georgie except my cousin's girlfriend, Alice. She caught us when we were seventeen in the basement getting frisky. We thought we were in deep manure, but she was okay with it. After Georgie died… everything just changed, and I put that part of me in the ground where no one could find it. They were the best years of my life, though."

"What are you saying?" Cody asked.

Rob tsked. "Don't be willfully stupid, kid. You see, every time I tried to say my name, it came out wrong. I always got stuck on the *B*s. Everyone called my Bobby back then. We figured it would be safer to correspond under an alias and have the letters sent to where Alice was staying at the time."

"Orange Blossom Drive," I muttered.

Rob tipped his head. "Alice rented a room from her friend there. The times… were different back then. We were branded sick, perverts and child molesters. It would be dangerous to come out."

"This doesn't make any sense," Cody said, his voice quaking. "I didn't even know you were gay."

The man took a big breath, then let it out slowly. "After I lost Georgie, I became someone else. He was the one, the love of a lifetime. The kind of love everyone dreams about but so few ever find. I tried moving on, but it didn't feel right. I took those years I had with him and locked them away in my heart. Then I became Rob and did everything we had talked about. Georgie talked about seeing Hawaii so many times. No one knew about us except for Alice, but she died a long time ago. To my family, I had simply lost a friend, but I felt as if a piece of me had been torn away."

As Rob went on talking about his life with Georgie, I found myself next to Cody, our hands entwined. Rob's eyes misted, but he was all smiles as he recounted their adventures as teenagers in the fifties. I had to force myself to breathe as I listened, my sole focus on the man I had come here to find. Was Bibby really sitting in front of me? It was like an old movie playing in 3-D, but Rob and Georgie's story was one that deserved to be on the silver screen.

"On some level, I thought I'd see him again, despite knowing the odds were against him coming home," he said, removing his glasses and pinching the bridge of his nose.

Cody sniffled.

"Christ, I forget you are leaky," Rob teased.

"I can't help it," Cody protested, scrubbing his face. "This is so much to take in…. Uncle—why didn't you ever tell me?"

The man was quiet for a few moments. He smiled ruefully. "Everyone has their secrets. Do you remember what I told you about dying alone?"

Cody nodded and proceeded to make a mess of himself. I couldn't stop the smile from arching over my lips. I felt beyond blessed to have been allowed into Rob's beautiful world. My eyes stung with tears, but it felt good.

Rob's attention fell on me. "Looks like I have another nephew to spoil."

I didn't know what to say to that, so I simply nodded.

"I held your mother once, when she was a baby. It was after Georgie died. She was the cutest thing. I tried to stay connected in some form to his family, but it was just another reminder of what I had lost. It was too painful to deal with, so I distanced myself from them," Rob said.

I couldn't say anything. This all seemed so unreal. I wanted to ask him for details, but he seemed equally as shocked. I realized how hard this must be for him.

"I'm sorry," I blurted. "For digging this all up again."

The man smiled faintly. "They say pain dulls in time. I call bullshit."

Gasping, Cody shot to his feet. "The letter!"

As realization smacked me in the head, I pointed at the envelope in Rob's hands, my words getting tangled. Rob looked at it, then frowned.

"This makes no sense," he said.

"It's dated the day he died," I stumbled to explain. "We don't think he was killed in action, he—"

"Read it, Uncle. Please. It's for you," Cody cut in.

We both held our breaths as Rob slid the paper out and unfolded it. The silence was deafening and seemed to crawl for hours. I held on to Cody's arm as Rob's eyes slid over the words. His face contorted in a variety of emotions—confusion, excitement… love. By the time he was done, tears were streaming down his plump cheeks. Cody was by his side in an instant, hugging him tightly.

I watched as he comforted his uncle, and though Rob was bawling uncontrollably, I knew they were tears of relief and joy. I could relate to the shadow that had no doubt hung over his head all these years—*Had Georgie still loved me when he died?*

I realized I would never have the closure Rob had. It would always haunt me that I never gave Mom the chance to know who I was, but I would live on, just like Rob had, and enjoy every minute of the rest of my life.

"I n-n-never faulted him," Rob said, running his hand across his cheek. "For wanting to leave me. He thought it would be better if I moved on. He seemed convinced it would be easier for me if I found a girl. I think… he kind of gave up on ever coming home."

"He chose you in the end, Uncle," Cody rasped. "I'm sorry it took you this long to know that."

CHAPTER SEVENTEEN

THE RIDE back to Cody's house was silent. Neither of us seemed to know what to say. My attention was constantly drawn to him as he ran his fingers through his hair. I could see the sheen in his eyes, the lingering tears letting me know we were both in a vulnerable mood. On some level, the last hour spent with Rob hadn't really happened. Happy endings were reserved for books and movies…. Weren't they?

He pulled up to his house and cut the engine, then looked at me. "Did that really just happen?"

"I think so," I croaked, my throat dry.

Cody stared out the window, wide-eyed. "You know, I never thought we'd actually find Bibby. I guess I romanticized the idea."

"Same."

"But oh my God!" he said, hitting the steering wheel. "He's been here all this time. I thought I knew my uncle well, but I never imagined he had this secret life. And… I guess I'm kind of disappointed he never shared it with me. Of all people, I thought he'd know I could understand. I don't know how to feel about that."

"We all have our secrets." I repeated Rob's words, watching the cattle frolicking in the snow. "We should be thankful he shared it with us now. He could have never said a thing about it."

"You're right, I suppose. I don't know. I'm in a really weird mood. I mean, where do we go from here?" Slowly, a smile curved over his lips. "Damn, Aiden. We have one helluva story to tell our kids someday."

I chuckled, liking that idea.

He took a deep breath and let it out slowly. "I'm being selfish, aren't I? I'm glad we managed to give my uncle some peace, and now he knows Georgie chose him in the end. That's all that counts. It's what we set out to do."

159

"It's hard to find that completeness," I mumbled, feeling strangely open.

He turned his attention to me, his gorgeous eyes glimmering. "That was a hell of a treasure hunt, wasn't it?"

"And it was entirely worth it," I said. "Though I'd have to say the journey was equally as exciting. With the world's best guide and all."

He grinned, his smile brightening the air around him. He glanced at his house, then returned his attention to me. "Want to come in?"

"Yep."

With that we were out of the car and in his bedroom in the flick of a cow's tail, our hands grasping for clothes, our lips fused. I just needed to get him naked and against me with nothing in between. I was raw and vulnerable, and Cody offered shelter.

Closing my eyes, I listened to his heartbeat and the flow of air through his lungs. His thumb stroked my side, and I'd never before felt more comfortable in my skin.

"About what I said earlier... coming up here, it wasn't about finding Bibby. Sure, that was a small part of it, but I just needed to get away from the congestion of my family. Put things into perspective. To be honest, I needed to find me."

"And did it work?"

"Yeah, I think it did. Nothing is ever perfect in life, but I refuse to live for someone else anymore. I can't go back and change not telling my mother who I really am, and I know I have to accept that. My father might come to accept me one day, but I can't mold my life around the hope that he will. Like you said before—I have to find what makes me happy."

"And that is?" he prompted, then pressed a kiss to my forehead.

I chuckled. "I should probably start with a job, considering I don't have one. I might go back to school for agriculture science.... It's something to think about, anyway. And I have to go home and deal with my mother's house. Hell, I might just follow Brian to Europe."

"Oh."

I craned my head up to regard Cody. His eyes were closed, his lashes pressed against his flushed cheeks. He was gorgeous in a heartbreaking way. Something painful stabbed my heart. I was going to miss this guy something fierce, but I couldn't stay here. It was time to be a big boy and stop running.

I relaxed and held him close, afraid to let go. His breath evened out as he drifted off to sleep. I realized leaving Valley Forge would be one of the hardest things I'd ever do.

"Have breakfast with me tomorrow before you go," he mumbled.

"Deal."

I COULDN'T pinpoint the exact moment I realized Cody was heartbroken to see me go. It might have been the expression he passed me when waking up from our nap... or the crack in his voice... or the way he watched me with longing as I packed my stuff. And though it made me feel all warm and fuzzy to know he cared about me, this was exactly what I had wanted to avoid.

I didn't want to hurt him. The realization I was going to tore me up.

"You got everything?" he asked as he checked the motel drawers.

"Cody—" I started, my voice sounding thin to my own ears.

"I knew this day was coming," he said simply as he headed for the door. "I knew it going in, so you don't have to explain. I just need you to promise me one thing, okay? Keep in touch. Send me an e-mail every now and then, or ring me. I consider you a friend, Aiden, and hope you do too."

I dropped my bag and yanked him into a suffocating hug, committing to memory the scent of his skin and the warmth of his body. His solidness kept me upright again. I was so close to staying, but I didn't want to fall into old habits of running from everything.

"You know," he said against my neck. "If you ever find yourself in the area and looking for a little nookie—"

"Shut up," I teased, holding him close. "And if you ever decide to take the plunge and visit Texas, I make mean cornbread."

"That you do."

Cody followed behind me as I steered the Hummer to Mama Hen's, where we had agreed to have breakfast. As usual, it was busy, the parking lot filled. I located a space and killed my engine, then met Cody at the entrance. He beamed at me, and I narrowed my eyes suspiciously.

"What?"

"Nothing," he said, shrugging. "Come on. I'm starving."

I followed him in and greeted Abby, who looked more enthusiastic to be working than she should. I was surprised by the hug she offered me, her lips turned up in a sly smile. She led us to the back, and I stopped in my tracks. Several tables had been pushed together, and a collection of a dozen balloons tied to a chair swayed gently. I gaped as Marge slammed into me.

"You didn't," I said against her shoulder.

Cody grinned victoriously and took a seat, looking smug.

"I drew this for you!" Jenny said, holding up a picture of me driving on the road.

I accepted it and thanked her.

As familiar but nameless people took their turns hugging the stuffing out of me, my cheeks started to ache, the joy of the room soaking into me. I'd never had so much attention come at me from so many directions that my head reeled. Warmth rose up in me, and I wanted to cry. I was going to miss Cody, but these people who had shown me nothing but kindness would stay with me for a long time.

"Not there." Cody stopped me before I could sit down.

He led me over to the chair with the balloons tied to it, and I accepted the seat. Chuckling, I said, "I feel like the birthday boy."

Abby came around and took our orders. As everyone chatted and asked questions about Texas, my gaze was constantly drawn to Cody. Surprisingly, he was quiet, chiming in every now and then when someone asked him something. I'd never seen him so despondent, but it didn't take a genius to figure out why.

I wished there was something I could do or say to cheer him up.

Mark, Jarome, and DeShawn arrived, and I banged fists with them. Their presence reinvigorated Cody, but the look of loss in his eyes was obvious. As breakfast turned into hours of conversation, I sat back against my chair, watching everyone interact.

Not only was I losing Cody, but I felt as if I was losing a family too. If I was lucky, I'd salvage what was left of the family I had back home, but I knew Dad and Missy would never share times like this with me.

My phone buzzed in my pocket. My first reaction was to ignore it, but I pulled it out and glanced at the screen. Frowning, I got up and found a quiet corner.

"Allie?"

"Aiden! Oh my God, where have you been? Your father called me, frantic. Told me you'd gotten drunk and disappeared? Everyone is looking for you—"

It was nice to hear my cousin's voice, no matter how worried she sounded. "No, that's not what happened. I mean, I got drunk, but… never mind. I'm not missing. I had to take care of something in Montana."

"Montana?" she gasped.

"It's a long story, one I hope to tell you soon. I'm okay. I'm not having a mental breakdown, contrary to what my father might have implied."

After a moment, she laughed. "He always did exaggerate. You are seriously okay? I know it's hard to lose the people you love. Justin asked me the other day if Audrey would be calling him from heaven. I don't think he completely understands the concept of death, and I don't have the heart to explain. She would call every week, and they would talk a good half hour about school and soccer."

I smiled, the thought warming. "I'm more than okay. For the first time in a very long time, I'm great. Amazing."

"That's so good to hear. Can I ask what inspired your change in mood? At the funeral you were… despondent."

I glanced to where everyone was commiserating, my eyes finding Cody chatting with Mark. "A guy."

Allie made a sound of confusion.

"I'm gay, Allie," I said, surprised how easy the words came, and I didn't bother to whisper either.

"Oh. Well… I didn't know. But that's fine. How was your Christmas? I tried calling but didn't get an answer. Now I know why."

I was a bit taken aback by the nonissue of my sexuality. I had expected her to ask all the basic questions—*Are you sure? How do you know?* But she seemed unfazed by the revelation. I realized how removed I was from my own family out of some misplaced fear, and the regret of hiding myself for so long slammed into me with the force of a linebacker.

"It was good. I made Mom's cornbread, and it was a hit. Allie, we need to get together sometime. We used to be close, and I miss that. Coming out here has made me see how important family is, and I want to hold on to what I have left."

"Aiden! You're breaking my heart! I would love that. I miss you so much. Do you remember when we used to make mud pies?"

I burst out in laughter, catching the attention of several people. "I actually tried to eat them."

She giggled, her voice beautiful. "We'll do that. We're only a state away, you know."

"Allie, can I ask you something?"

"Sure."

"Do you remember Uncle Georgie? Mom mentioned him a few times," I asked carefully.

"Oh sure. If you recall, my dad is something of a history buff. Talked about Georgie's service in the war. What about him?"

I opened my mouth, but my brain stalled. I was still too raw from the emotions Rob had dug up to go into detail. I settled for simple truth. "I found some of his stuff in the attic and was wondering how he died. There wasn't a death certificate."

"Oh my gosh! Dad told me about it. It is so sad, Aiden. Apparently he was killed by a crane on the docks while preparing to sail home. Can you imagine surviving the horrors of war only to be crushed to death on your way home? It still bothers me to this day. I was always a big sap for things like that."

My heart caught in my throat as she talked. I thought I would be relieved to have the final puzzle piece, but it was just another reminder of the loss Rob had suffered. And it shattered the last thread holding me to this place. Our conversation came to an end with me promising to get together with her soon.

I returned to my seat to find a piece of chocolate cake waiting for me. Marge told me, since I wouldn't be around for them to celebrate my birthday, she was taking the opportunity to do so now. I couldn't help thinking of Mom and Marge becoming the best of friends. They would have gotten along great.

As afternoon loomed, everyone started leaving. I accepted many more rounds of hugs and kind words and well-wishes in my journeys. Cody's dad made me promise to take good care of the arrowhead, and I happily obliged.

"You take care of yourself, Aiden. Do you hear?" Marge said, crushing me to her. "Make yourself intrusive and visit us sometime."

"I will try," I said honestly.

"And you," she said, patting Cody on his cheek. "I expect to see you at the fair later."

"Yes, Mom."

When everyone was gone, I inquired, "Fair?"

"Just a little New Year's gathering," he explained, walking beside me as we left the restaurant. "She usually bakes this huge, extravagant cake."

I blinked at him, caught off guard. I hadn't realized the New Year had snuck up on me so stealthily.

"Oh, I almost forgot. Uncle Rob told me to tell you you'd better keep in touch with him if you know what's good for you—

his words. He wanted to be here, but well… I don't think I need to explain that one."

I nodded, finding myself at a loss for words. I wanted to tell Cody how thankful I was for all his help… what he meant to me. He'd opened my eyes to a whole other world I hadn't known existed and shown me wonders no wealthy man could buy with money. He deserved so much more than I could express, and a simple thank-you didn't seem appropriate.

"Well, guess it's time to hit the road, huh?" he said ruefully.

I tugged him toward me and wrapped him in a hug. His arms tightened around me until I couldn't breathe. His scent was lovely, and I focused on it, stamping it into my brain. I was terrified that the memory of this amazing guy would fade, that I would forget what it felt like to lie naked with him, the way his lips slid against mine. Just as the pain faded to manageable levels, so too would he, no matter how much I wanted it otherwise, and that fact nearly shattered me.

Before I broke down, I pulled away and forced a smile onto my face. "It's been thrilling."

"I know. I'm good like that," he teased.

I grinned. We stood staring at each other for a long moment. I managed to find a shred of courage. "All right, I better get going. I've got a long drive ahead."

I was aware of Cody watching my every move as I pulled out of the parking lot. He waved, and I returned the gesture, his face bright. It took a lot to hit the pedal, and as my car glided down the street, I kept checking my mirror. Cody stayed in view until the road turned.

Setting my attention in front of me, I stiffened my muscles to keep my foot right where it was.

Leaving Valley Forge hurt nearly as much as saying good-bye to Mom.

CHAPTER EIGHTEEN

I HAD only been on the road for two hours, but every second seemed like an eternity. As I neared the Montana-Wyoming border, the mountains seemed to follow me like pale ghosts of memories determined to remind me they existed. My gaze was constantly drawn to my rearview mirror. The road was clear of snow, and I laid it on the pedal, determined to escape the mountains. As the car accelerated, I rolled down the windows. The chilled air rushed into the cab, stinging my face and jostling my hair. As someone who took little risk and obeyed speed limits, it was awesome to be so free and reckless.

I spotted the highway patrol car but didn't back off. Instead I pressed it to ninety, and I thought I might just take off to the sky. No surprise, the cop pulled out and flashed his lights. Sighing, I slowed down and pulled to the side. The rush had been great but short-lived. I remained polite to his gentle chastisement and offered my paperwork. He returned a few minutes later with a ticket in hand.

"Roads are slick this time of the year. I was your age once and get the thrill of speeding, but you don't want to end up as roadkill now, do you?"

I thanked him and watched as he left. I dropped my eyes to the ticket and chortled openly until I hiccupped. Jobless, I was going to have to be mindful of spending money, and that included speeding tickets. I still had several thousands of dollars' worth of medical bills to pay off, as well as student loans. I let the slip of paper flutter to the passenger seat.

Sitting back, I stared at the open road in front of me, the asphalt snaking in the distance and cutting through a flat and mountainless terrain. It made me think of that thing Bilbo had said about the road going ever on. Mom had read the story to me when I was four. She would sit with me in bed, and we would read a few pages every night. It had taken us two months to get through the book, but I could remember falling asleep to her lilting voice as she changed her tone to mimic the characters. Strange, but I had forgotten about that until now. After all these years, that memory still lived deep inside.

Somewhere out there past the plains, Mom was buried in the ground and Dad was playing house with his new wife. The farmhouse and the windmills and the now-barren cornfields... straight in front of me was familiarity and safety. Suddenly it felt a lot less cozy, like a hearth going out in the dead of winter, dread following behind the slowly chilling air.

I scrubbed my face, then got out. I stretched my legs and tried to keep from glancing at the mountains, but they had a way of commanding my attention. They pulled at me like a magnet, urging me toward them... and back to Valley Forge. After several long minutes of just blinking at them, I came to the conclusion that I was drawn to what they represented—*change*... and the fear of it. Going back to Texas to deal with the farmhouse and my family was familiar. Hiding who I was and accepting the way things were with Dad and Missy was safe. But to the north, in Valley Forge with Cody and his family, was an adventure just waiting for me to walk that path. He promised a life of joy and love, complete with all the trimmings of a real family.

If I stayed with Cody, would I be running away? Standing in the center of two possibilities, I didn't think so. Change was hard to accept, but trying to run from that change was cowardly. I told myself I needed to stop running, but here I was, doing just that.

You have to find what makes you happy. I swore I could hear Cody's words as if he were standing next to me. Could I leave behind everything I had ever known and be happy with Cody and his family? Leaving for college and going off to a strange city had been unsettling, but this was... terrifying.

168

What was I running from, though? I looked back toward the south, the horizon seeming bleak and cold. I know I needed to make an attempt to fix the problems with Dad and Missy, but I wasn't going to sacrifice my happiness for their idea of morality. The only question was… did Cody want the same? Everything told me that he did, from his longing glance to the frailty in his voice as he bid me good-bye. I wished he would have told me—but this was for me to figure out, I supposed. Maybe he had known that.

I stabbed my fingers into my hair and pulled. My sinuses swelled again, and I wanted to let loose. Everything was so complicated and yet simple.

I hopped back in the Hummer and kicked the car into gear. Throwing up dirt and old snow, I spun around and headed north. Despite my excitement of chasing change, I kept my speed at sixty-five. I didn't want to get pulled over again and delay getting back to Valley Forge.

The two-hour drive back to the town seemed even longer than it had leaving. I knew I should have tried phoning Cody, but my cell was in the backseat somewhere, and I wasn't going to stop for anything. Besides, I knew where he was. I caught sight of the motel and pulled into the parking lot. As I raced into the office, my heart was beating a billion miles an hour, and I was trembling from both exhilaration and fear.

The girl's face brightened as she spotted me. "Hey, I thought you were—"

"Where is the fair?" I demanded. "The New Year's party."

I listened intently as she detailed directions. Then I was out the door like Taz. All I could think about was getting to Cody and pulling him close to me. I pushed the speed limit, mindful of the slick ground. After double-parking the Hummer, I rushed into the old theater where the party was being held. Politely pushing my way through the crowd, I ran my eyes over the scene. I spotted Marge and made directly for her, my heart pounding with every step.

Her eyes brightened, and her cheeks plumped as she smothered me in a hug. "Did you forget something, hon?"

"Where is Cody?" I barked.

She frowned. "He isn't here yet. He said he had some work to do with his blog. Are you returning to the house? Please tell him if he isn't here in a half hour, I'm going to be very mad. Mad, not sad—"

I passed her an apologetic smile, then darted out of the theater. I strung sentences in my mind as I drove to the Bannar residence. I had no idea how to explain to Cody what I had figured out. Hell, I wasn't sure what it was myself. The only thing I did know was that it felt *right*. Just as Bibby and Georgie had felt right about their love, staying in Valley Forge with Cody was… *everything*.

The house was apparently empty. I knocked on every door and window but received no response. Figuring Cody was at his apartment, I hit the gas so hard the wheels spun, spitting out dirt. Banging on the door, I called his name.

The door shot open, and Jules looked at me from behind red-rimmed eyes. He frowned.

"Is Cody here?" I huffed, trying to catch my breath.

Jules shrugged. "I haven't seen him since this morning. I thought he was at the party. Didn't you leave this afternoon?"

I didn't answer, just took several steps back. Perhaps Cody was with his friends? But I had no idea where they lived, nor did I know their numbers. As I scanned the darkening land dotted with cattle, my heart began to fall. What was I thinking? My entire decision to come back was based on Cody wanting me. What if he considered me a friend but didn't see a future with me?

This isn't the first time you acted without thinking, I told myself.

When I settled my eyes on the edge of the forest, I gasped. I took a step forward, then another and another until I penetrated the woods. I wasn't sure if it was the winter air or my nerves, but I shivered as I made my way toward the covered bridge. When the trees ended, I stepped onto the overgrown road and looked into the bridge's maw, the beams creating a symmetrical pattern. It reminded me of a tunnel stemming from the darkest parts of the world, the beams a stepladder leading up into the light.

He's not here. Why would he be, anyway? Every step I took was torture. A part of me wanted him not to be there so I could turn around and go back to Texas and my safe, boring little world. The other….

The symmetry was interrupted as I penetrated the bridge. It took me a moment to realize someone was leaning over the guardrail, their jean-covered behind sticking out between the beams. As I drew closer, the wheat-colored hair of Cody's head popped out at me, and my heart kicked against my rib cage. His eyelashes fluttered as he gazed down on the frozen creek. He looked agonizingly beautiful, but under his demeanor was sadness, and I knew I had caused it.

A squeaky board gave me away, and he shot up, his eyes widening as he took me in. His mouth worked for a moment.

"Aiden? What—did you forget something?"

I nodded and came closer, every detail of his face coming into light despite the darkening sky. My approach was slow and steady, and my ears drummed with my own heartbeat. His gorgeous eyes flared as I leaned in. The moment I connected with his lips, a soothing warmth spread through me to chase away the cold. He responded, his little moan melodic to my ears. I knew he had been taken by surprise, but I didn't give him the chance to back away. I held him securely to me, his heat sinking deep into my bones as I stroked his tongue with mine in smooth, slow waves.

I was the first to back away. As intimate as this moment was, I knew he was owed an explanation.

"I don't understand," Cody whispered.

I bit my lip, my eyes darting all over his face. His expression reflected confusion, and his glassy baby blues searched me for answers. I could see the hope flaring, the possibility rising.

"I… I've come to understand that it wasn't my mother's death that had shattered me, but that I was trying to hide my true self all these years. I feel like a bucket, all the problems slowly trickling in until I can't hold any more. It was bound to spill over, and her passing was that final drop."

Cody's lips parted, but he couldn't seem to find any words.

I took his hand in mine, his skin warm and soft against my own. I circled his knuckle with the pad of my finger, tracing a tiny scar. "I don't want to run anymore. I want to be happy. You told me I need to figure out what makes me happy, and I have. It's this place. And the people. But most importantly, you make me happy. I'm aware we haven't known each other very long, but you've opened my eyes. I see things differently now. And we found Bibby together. He's a part of me, and so are you."

It became hard for me to speak, my head tightening and my eyes stinging with tears. I didn't bother to hold them back. There was so much I wanted to say, but I needed to pace myself, lest I implode. Cody seemed to understand, and he pulled me in, his arms holding me tight against him as if he were afraid I'd leave again. I fell against him, and the feeling of his fingers gliding across my scalp was heavenly. I cried openly against his neck, the release of pent-up sorrow lovely.

After a long moment of melting, I straightened my spine and dried my face. Clearing my throat, I decided to make my intentions clear. "I want to give this a shot if you want to. No matter your decision, I needed you to know that I care about you. I needed to be honest about my feelings for you."

I couldn't look at him. I was afraid to see his face twist as he tried to let me down gently. Putting one's heart on the line was never easy, but with everything happening in my life, I was sure the organ would be left on the ground in tatters.

His touch startled me, his fingers skimming across my cheek. He guided me into another kiss, his lips sliding against my own like a reassuring touch.

His voice was hardly more than a whisper. "I know you needed to figure out things on your own. I don't know how it happened or why… but you got me. I tried to keep a distance between us, but hell. I'm a big teddy bear, and I love everyone."

A smile creased my face, the analogy spot-on.

"Do you know what you are doing?" he prompted.

I nodded. "I'm doing something that makes me happy."

He seemed to want to refute my words, but I cut him off with a kiss. He pulled me closer and deepened the kiss, his tongue asking permission. I gave it to him, opening fully and letting him take the lead. My fingers grasped for purchase as I pushed him against the beam.

"Fuck," he whispered harshly. His fingers dipped under my jeans to grip my ass, the little points of pain wonderful.

Before I realized what was happening, he was leading me back toward his house, his fingers entwined with mine. I struggled to keep up, but when he turned and gave me a dazzling smile, I got my legs moving. He didn't take me to the house or his apartment but made a sharp turn when we exited the tree line. He led me directly into a barn, then pushed me down on a pile of hay.

I giggled as he straddled me, his fingers working at my coat. I found his lips again and claimed them, his tongue meeting my own in a frantic dance. When my coat was loosened, he undid my pants and gripped my cock securely. I arched up into his touch, the pressure perfect. I busied my hands, splitting his button-up, then undoing his jeans, and then we were entwined, our dicks against one another.

He rocked into me with purpose, and I wrapped a leg around his hips to keep him flush against me. Though we were mostly dressed and the air was crisp and cool, I was burning, a hungry fire raging inside of me. It didn't take long for us to achieve orgasm, and the barn was filled with our groans as we unloaded onto each other's bodies. I kept my eyes on him the entire time. Every detail cemented itself into my mind, from the way his lip curled up to the coloring in his cheeks.

It was like glimpsing into heaven, if ever such a place truly existed.

Chapter Nineteen

I LISTENED to Cody's heartbeat as it slowly evened out. His skin was hot and slick against my ear, and the scent of his body a roar in my nose. I held on to him, afraid he might try to move away, but he relaxed, his fingers playing in my hair. As the haze of pleasure slowly retreated, I closed my eyes.

"Well… I never did it on a haystack before. That was fun," Cody teased.

I grinned. "Oh, so you have done it in a barn but not on a haystack? Let me guess… the rafters." His silence confirmed my suspicions, and I landed a little spank to his thigh. "Oh, you naughty boy."

"Technically it was a blowjob," he said sheepishly. "And technically we haven't gone all the way on a haystack, but I'm hoping you might like to correct that with me. We can do the rafters too."

I chuckled, his suggestion that we had a future both exciting and endearing. Still, I was afraid to push the whole thing too far too quickly. Sex wasn't the same as intimacy, and he hadn't exactly confirmed he wanted to build a life with me.

"Has anything changed yet?" Cody asked, his question startling me.

I looked up at him to find his half-mast eyes on me. A straw of hay stuck out from the corner of his mouth, and it was jostling around as if he were decimating it. I slid it from his lips, and he blushed.

"You have a whole other life and a family in Texas. I can't ask you to give that up for me, no matter how much I want you to."

"You do?" I blurted as I scooted up his body to face him. "I mean, you want me to stay?"

174

He took a deep breath, then slowly let it out. "Yeah, I do. I'm just going to stop dancing around the issue and say it—I've fallen in love with you, Aiden. I guess I'm afraid you will stay here for a little while, then decide it's not what you want. I don't want any of us to end up brokenhearted. It's a big deal uprooting your life and leaving everything you've known behind. It's scary and confusing, and it's easier to run from that fear than face it."

"Says the little boy that got taken away?" I inquired. "I'm sorry. I didn't mean that to come out the way it did."

"No, it's okay. I know what you meant. And I suppose you're right. Not only that, but I've lived in fear for a long time that those who say they love me might one day leave or return me. I know it's a childish thought, but I'm working on getting past that. I just don't want to end up hurt when you move on."

His words made my throat tighten. I hated that he was intimate with the feeling of abandonment, and I was angry with myself for digging up unpleasant emotions. But I realized he had the same emotional protection tendencies as I did.

He eyed me closely. "Don't you dare go there! Yes, you leaving hurt, but it wasn't your fault. I knew going into this with you that it was a possibility. It was hard to watch you drive off, but I had accepted it. Honestly, I didn't expect you to return, but you are here and…. Jesus. Will this really work?"

"I will be honest. I can't stay here indefinitely. I have responsibilities in Texas. I have to sign contracts with the energy company, and Mom's house has to be taken care of. I was thinking of renting it out to low-income families. The mortgage was paid off years ago, and the money from the windmills pays for the property taxes. I can't live there. Not because everything will remind me of Mom, but staying there will keep me stuck in place. I have to move on and start living, and not for my father or anyone else. I also have to take care of my place in New York. Considering I no longer work for the company, I'm going to have to break the lease."

He seemed pleased with my declaration, his face softening as he ran a finger along my jaw. I couldn't believe the words were coming so easily to me, but I wasn't going to miss this opportunity. "After that is done, I would like to settle here. I'll need to get a job… maybe your father can teach me the ropes of cattle ranching."

"That all sounds really… nice," he said on a sigh.

"But," I finished for him.

Shaking his head, he looked away. I guided him back to me and kissed his lips gently. "I know it's easy to talk big. But standing up to my father and coming out here was hard. Leaving you on that corner was excruciating. The easiest option for me was to go back to Texas to everything I know. But I can't do that anymore. I'm not the man my father wants me to be, and I never will be. Standing on the road, I realized that that's okay."

His throat shifted, and his eyes shone with lodged tears. I realized he was waiting for me. I cleared my throat, the words flowing effortlessly. "I love you."

The corner of his lips twitched. "Don't tell me what you think I want to hear."

"You're an impossible person not to love. You are someone I aspire to be, Cody. Someone who genuinely cares about other people and does what he can to make their lives a little better. You are my personal hero." I took his hand in mine, watching the way our fingers entwined. They fit so perfect together. "But I don't want to walk this new path alone."

His fingers dug into my back, and he pulled me close. I felt his lips pressed atop my head, and his breath brushed across my forehead.

"Besides…. Bibby lives here, and I would really like to get to know him too. I feel as if he is a huge part of my life. I mean, if it wasn't for his letters, I never would have left, and I would have never met you. This is what I want, Cody. I've never been so sure in my life."

"I want you to stay," he said, and he made a tiny sound that let me know he was crying.

Beaming, I looked up at him and wiped a tear from his cheek. "You sap."

He laughed, the sound beautiful. "I am. Are you prepared to deal with all my leaks?"

"Yup... all of them."

"Oh, who is the naughty boy now?"

I growled low in my throat and claimed his lips. He responded, his tongue running across mine in seductive sweeps.

He broke off suddenly. "Hey, I have an idea. You need a job... you're good with the important stuff, right? Like records and money and smart investing? I do well with my blog, but I have to spend several hours a week trying to keep track of everything like royalties and e-mails from fans. Maybe you can help me with that. Like... manage that stuff so I can focus on content. I would pay you a salary of course. If you want to, anyway."

"You know, that sounds like fun," I said, truly intrigued by the idea. I wanted to be a better man like Cody, and what better way to start than getting into his line of work?

He nearly jumped to his feet, his expression brightening. "I'm going back with you to Texas. I mean, I've wanted to take my blog on the road forever. Meet people, talk to them, and hear what they have to say. It would be so much fun.... I'm getting ahead of myself, aren't I?"

I cuddled him close to me, not wanting him to get away in his excitement. "I would like that. We can do a travelogue too."

"Oh yeah! Aiden! We have to do this," he said. He talked until he ran out of breath, detailing ideas for visiting landmarks. "Really? You want me to come back with you?"

"You have to see Texas eventually, remember?" I said.

"I know, but... I will only come if it's what you want."

I blinked at him, still taken aback by his compassion and kindness. "I don't think I could do it alone. I want you there with me."

"This is going to be so much fun! Can you imagine all the cool things we will see and the awesome people we'll get to talk to? I can't wait."

His enthusiasm was infectious, and images of us traveling together invaded my mind.

"Of course, we'll have to have sex in every city," he said, his voice dropping.

A chuckle bubbled up. I did like the sound of that. We lay on top of the haystack for a long time, his arms holding me close to him. I could see through the cracks in the wood that it had gotten late, the sun long since set.

"Are you cold?" Cody asked, tugging my coat over my exposed belly.

"No."

"Good. Because I don't want to move."

After a long moment, I said, "Your mom is going to kill us."

He laughed. "She will understand."

CHAPTER TWENTY

Several weeks later…

"AND HERE we are!" Cody exclaimed as he got out of my Hummer and pointed the camera lens at his face. "Tex-ass! Home of… cattle and the cowboys and Republicans. But we made it. And look, Aiden is with us. Say hello, babe."

I smiled shyly and waved awkwardly as he pointed the camera in my direction. Cody had stayed glued to his recorder, documenting everything during the drive from Montana to Texas. It had taken us two weeks to drive through four states, but I had loved every minute of it. True to his words, we'd seen so many amazing things and spent many hours talking with people, some of which were his fans. I had tried to stay out of the way, but Cody would pull me in. I knew it was an old habit to keep myself out of the spotlight, but I was working on being more involved with his job.

Cody grinned into the camera. "He's still really shy, but we're working on that, aren't we?"

He turned to span the cornfields, talking to the camera about windmills and how they were good for energy but bad for wildlife. During our journey, Uncle Rob had called, demanding details on our travels. He had even directed us to some things to see. We had talked briefly, but the whole thing with Georgie was still too fresh for him, and I didn't push it. I could sense he wanted to share that part of his life with us, but he wasn't ready. He seemed ecstatic that Cody and I had hit it off, though, and made me promise to take good care of his nephew.

Cody flipped the camera closed, then regarded me. "Sorry, I'm getting carried away. I can't believe I'm finally in Texas. It's kind of exciting."

He marched up to me and wrapped his arms around my hips, pulling me close to him. He planted a soft kiss on my lips and ran a hand up and down my arm. I leaned into him, running my nose against his cheek and inhaling.

"You're feeling it now, aren't you?" he asked gently.

There was no need for him to clarify—I knew exactly what he meant. I nodded. "I have a lot of memories here. Some bad, many good. These last few weeks have been one hell of a distraction, and I will admit I purposely lost myself in them. But now I'm back, it's like being hit with a fire hose."

"I'm here for you, Aiden. Whatever you need, you let me know. Understand?" Cody asked, his tone even and smooth, and his expression let me know he was serious. "I know it's hard to have your father and sister disapprove of your choices, but if they love you, they will learn to accept it. Just give it some time."

I smiled, because joy fluttered against my heart despite the lingering sorrow. When I had told Dad what my plans were for the house and my life, he hadn't been happy and had accused Cody of manipulating me with his "perversions." His words had hurt, but Cody seemed unfazed.

Cody took my hand and gently pulled me with him. I was surprised to find how easy I took that first step and every one after that. He guided me up the porch and to the front door.

I dug my keys out and said, "I forgot to show you my whale box. Remind me to do that later."

"Okay."

The front door was a lot lighter than I remembered, and when we were inside, Cody ran his eyes all over my mother's belongings. Everything sat quietly in its place, and the calming tick-tick of the cuckoo clock filled the silence. He turned his attention toward the stairs and tugged. I followed, his hand secure against my own. I showed him my room first, and he wagged his brows at me suggestively.

"Well, we've christened every hotel room from Montana to Texas, so I guess it's only right that we do the same here," I said.

Cody knew me so well already, his lecherous expression evening out. *No stalling, no more avoiding the inevitable.* I was the first to move and guided him back out into the hall. My mother's peach door loomed, and as I approached, it didn't seem to move farther away like it had the last time I was here. The knob was cool but not frigid, and I turned it, then pushed the door open. When we were inside, I closed my eyes, Mom's perfume heavy in the air. It was both comforting and heartbreaking.

Cody squeezed my hand, reminding me he was with me every step of the way. I was glad he had followed me to Texas, because I was sure I wouldn't have been able to do this without him.

"I can do this," I said. "I was thinking I could donate most of her furniture and clothes to a charity shop. I plan to keep only the things that were dearest to her... like the duck toilet paper dispenser."

He arched a brow at me, and I chuckled.

"I think that is a good idea."

"I need you to push me, though. I want to keep everything, because the idea of letting everything... letting *her* go is excruciating."

"I promise," he said and wrapped an arm around my waist. I leaned against him again, needing his support. "But we can't do anything today. It's almost six."

I turned and blinked at him, then muttered an expletive. We were supposed to have arrived yesterday but had gotten sidetracked sightseeing. During our road trip, Darnell had called and convinced me to have dinner with him to discuss some matters. I thought it was odd, but I didn't question it, nor had I thought about it until this moment.

We scrambled to get our significant luggage into the house, then took a shower together. The urge to fool around was tempting, but we refrained. I was glad Cody knew when I needed a little guidance, and he didn't hesitate to whip my butt into shape.

The drive out to Darnell's residence wasn't very long, because his house was on the edge of the city. I was shocked by the grandeur, the Victorian-style two-story situated against a well-manicured lawn and a flourishing garden. I supposed working for an energy company paid well.

I had yet to decide what I wanted to do with my life, but Cody had expressed support of me going back to school, and we had glanced at some colleges in Montana together. In the meantime, I helped him get his records straight and organized his priorities regarding the blog business. Reading all his fan mail was the highlight, though, and I was amazed by the amount of people he had touched. I had seemed to earn a few fans during our travels as well, and Cody had asked if I would like to share my story with others. I thought it was a good idea, but I wasn't ready and promised to tell him when I was.

We walked to the front door, our hands united. It was hard to say when my shift in perspective had occurred, but I no longer feared people realizing I was gay. I had come to learn most didn't care, and those few who passed me an annoyed look failed to evoke any sort of negative feelings from me. As Cody had said, people were going to disapprove of something or other, and we couldn't live our lives by their standards.

Darnell answered the door promptly, a big smile on his face. Dressed in a pair of fine slacks and a dress shirt, he looked every bit the businessman. He dropped his eyes to our hands for a moment, and I introduced Cody as my boyfriend. I had to admit, that word on my lips sounded awesome.

He seemed unfazed and invited us in. The interior was equally as extravagant as the outside, with polished oak furniture and photographs encased in silver frames. Despite the affluent air, a gentleness radiated outward—this was a *home*, a place touched by the warmth of a real family.

I accepted Darnell's palm, his handshake firm.

"I hope your drive was good?" he asked.

"It was very… eventful," I said, and I caught Cody fighting a smile out of the corner of my eye.

"Good. I'm glad." When a young woman in her early twenties appeared behind Darnell, he gasped and guided her forward. "This is my daughter, Tiara."

"It's nice to meet you," Tiara said, exchanging a hug with me and Cody. "Dinner should be ready soon."

Darnell passed her an uneasy look, then turned back to me. "While we wait, would it be okay if we took a seat in the front room? As I told you on the phone, there are some things I wanted to discuss with you."

"Sure." When we were settled, I said, "Like I said before, I am happy to sign any paperwork to keep the windmills operational. Since the property was handed down to me—"

"No, that's not why I invited you here," he said, his body stiff as he leaned forward. He ran a finger across his upper lip, as if he were unsure of how to proceed. "When I talked to you at your mother's funeral, I wasn't completely honest."

I passed a look at Cody, and he shrugged.

Darnell took a deep breath. "My relationship with Audrey was… complicated. Yes, we met while securing the contract for the mills, but…. Lord, give me strength. I can't think of any other way to say this. Your mother and I were involved."

I blinked at him, waiting for clarification. His words swirled around me in a tornado of confusion. As I took in every inch of him, from the short gray curls at his temples to his full lips, I realized why he looked familiar. I had seen him before in passing. *Where?* It was on the edge of my mind, the memory buried by grief and anger, but it was there. The mental image was blurry, like a picture slowly being fished out from the sea, coming into focus as it was revealed.

Sighing, he scratched the back of his neck. "I know this might come as a shock to you, but we were together for three years."

The memory slammed into me, and I blurted, "Doritos."

Cody tossed me the side-eye, but Darnell smiled tightly. "You remember, good."

A week before I had pulled the plug, I had retreated to the break room after an argument with Missy. Frustrated with her insistence to let Mom die and my own cowardice to do what was necessary, I had taken my sorrow out on the vending machine after my bag of chips had gotten stuck. A man had been nice enough to feed the machine some money and request what I had, pushing my bag out. It had been this man… Darnell.

"You were there visiting her?" I asked, agape.

"I tried to be as discreet as possible, but you were always at her bedside. Many times I had wanted to introduce myself, but I figured it was the wrong time. I… I suppose I expected her to survive."

"Wait… you were involved with Mom, like *romantically*?"

My words seemed to unnerve him, and he tugged on his collar. "I understand this is hard for you to accept, considering we come from different worlds. Audrey wanted to tell you many times, but she was afraid of how you might react."

"Because you are black," I deduced, and he fidgeted.

As the implications hit me, my sinuses grew tight, and I shook my head in denial. I couldn't believe Mom hadn't trusted me enough to tell me she was in love with this man. Cody took my hand, his squeeze comforting. I took a deep breath, then let it out. She had done the exact same thing as I had. We had hidden ourselves from each other out of misplaced fear. I couldn't be upset with her for that. Still, it was shattering.

Pulling the tears back, I croaked, "I wish she would have told me."

"I'm sorry you had to find out this way. She did want to tell you many times but was afraid. Audrey was a remarkable woman, and I sincerely hope this doesn't change your opinion—"

"Don't even do that," I hissed. I quickly reined myself in. I could see from Darnell's expression that he believed her fears were justified, and it speared my heart to realize my father's influence had dictated more than just my life. I tried to imagine what Mom must have felt every time she talked to me, the persistent need to

184

tell her son she had found someone who loved her, only to keep it in for fear of rejection. *Guilt. Regret. Pain.*

I shot to my feet, and Darnell rose to meet me. "I wish she would have told me about your relationship, but not because you are black. It hurts that she kept this part of her life from me, but I understand. And I am grateful that she wasn't alone, that she had someone to spend her life with."

He seemed blown away, his eyes widening, and his mouth worked like a fish's. Shaking his head, he slowly sat back down. "I imagined this going so many different ways, but never like this."

"Because my father is a racist and a bigot," I said, and putting the facts into words did a lot to cement my resolve. "And he affected more than just my life, it seems."

I sank back down next to Cody, who had remained silent the entire time, but his presence was keenly felt, and his quiet support fueled me on.

Darnell nodded, his voice cracking. "Audrey had told me about him and his viewpoints on certain matters. Even then I believed her fear to hide our relationship from you was due to his influence, but I suppose I was scared as well. She talked about you all the time and how proud of you she was. She also told me she was terrified of your relationship changing if you knew and shared your father's opinions."

As he talked, my head swelled and my throat tightened. So much heartache had come from misunderstandings. An image of Darnell and my mother together flashed in my mind. I would have loved to be involved with them... and I would have loved to have Mom know Brian for what he really was to me. It was hard not to be bitter about the whole thing. A tear escaped, and I quickly wiped it away.

"I'm sorry. I know this is so soon after... but it has been weighing heavily on me. You deserved to know, and truthfully, I had been wanting to meet you for a while now."

"No, that's not why.... It's just it's me all over again. I kind of hid myself from Mom too, and the regret of not being able to tell her the truth nearly destroyed me."

185

Darnell's eyes flashed to Cody for an instant before returning to me. "You mean about being gay? Your mother suspected. She had confided in me about her suspicions and was certain you would tell her when you were ready."

I gaped, sure I had misunderstood him. "She knew? But—did she think—?"

"She didn't care. She was adamant about that. She loved you, Aiden, and nothing could have changed that," Darnell said, sounding so certain.

I shook my head, wanting to deny his words. Cody ran a hand up and down my back as I sniffled. I scrubbed my face, the pressure inside my chest sharp. This wasn't fair. All this time we had been hiding things from each other out of some silly, misplaced fear. Opportunities had been missed… experiences denied. I wanted to blame everything on my father, but I knew it wasn't completely his fault.

"Sorry to bother you," Tiara said carefully as she stood at the doorjamb. "Dinner is ready."

Darnell shot to his feet and took her hand, urging her into the room. Her eyes were wide, her face twisted by uncertainty.

"Aiden… I hope in time that we might get to know each other. I loved your mother dearly and want to know the man she talked so highly of. And I would like you to know me and my daughter. But if this is too hard for you, I understand."

I looked back and forth between them, my attention settling on Darnell. I could see the pain in his eyes and knew well the ache my mother's death had brought to him. He had put a lot on the line to tell me the truth and risk his emotions. I managed to get to my feet, my steps shaky as I inched closer to him.

I held out my palm in a gesture of solidarity, my hand vibrating from nerves. "I would like that."

Darnell let go of his daughter and pulled me into a hug, slapping me on the back. Just like that, the tension and sorrow eased. When we parted, he smiled and pulled Tiara back against him. Though it was premature, I felt as if I were gaining another family in addition to the Bannars.

She gasped, looking behind me. "Would you like me to get you a tissue?"

I followed her attention and grinned. Cody was in tears, and he waved her away. *The big sap*, I teased silently.

"I'm fine, really. This happens all the time. But I'm starving, and my stomach will be sad if it doesn't get a taste of whatever smells so good."

We all sat down at the table and shared a pork roast. Darnell and Tiara shared stories with me about Mom and their life together. I told them about Cody and how we met. Tiara and Cody chatted endlessly, the two having a lot in common. The hours flew by as stories, both happy and sad, were exchanged. Sometimes a tear was shed, other times laughter filled the dining room. Finally the evening came to a close, and Darnell and Tiara walked us to the front door.

"Please, keep in touch," Darnell said, pulling away from a hug.

"Absolutely. I will be moving to Montana with Cody, but I would like to do this again sometime. I will be in town for a week or so while I deal with Mom's house. Maybe we can do something next weekend?"

"That would be great!" The man beamed. "You have my number. Just call. Weekends are always good for me."

I was surprised how hard I found it to leave. Darnell and his daughter stood in the doorway waving as we drove off. When we rounded the block, I sighed and reached for Cody's hand. His palm met mine, and our fingers entwined.

"Are you okay?" he asked.

"Jesus Christ, did that actually happen?" I said on a big expulsion of air. "But yeah. I so am."

"Good."

I knew the guilt and pain born from not telling Mom the truth would always be there, but it would lessen in time. Knowing she hadn't been alone all these years, that she had been happy with Darnell and Tiara, helped ease that realization. The biggest relief was her suspicion of my orientation and apparent unconcern. I was certain she'd known I had loved her, and I knew she had loved me.

A memory raced to the front, one of the many where I had sat at her bedside, begging her to wake up. That night I had decided to let her go, I had apologized profusely, sobbing all over myself. I let her know I hoped I was doing the right thing and told her how much I loved her. Her finger had twitched then, just the barest pressure against my knuckle. The doctor had told me it was common for the body to move, but I needed to believe she had known I was there… that she had heard me. I had never been one to believe in God, but I was sure our consciousness continued to exist in some form or another.

As we headed back toward Mom's house, I took a sharp turn at the last minute. Cody cursed and grabbed on to the seat, his eyes wide as he looked at me in disbelief. I had no time to explain, though. It was nearly closing time, but I needed to do this. As I drove through the cemetery gates, Cody quieted.

I found the section that housed Mom's grave and killed the engine. Taking a steadying breath, I stepped out and onto the grass. Cody was by my side in an instant, and I took his hand. Though I had been mentally absent during her burial, I knew where to go. The patch of grass, slightly lighter than the rest, guided me, and I knelt down in front of her headstone. I tugged Cody down with me and traced the etched letters of her name.

"Hey, Mom," I managed, my voice shaky. "I want you to meet someone. This is Cody, my boyfriend."

I had heard talking to lost loved ones could be therapeutic, but my words sounded crazy to my ears. But I needed to do this.

"Hey, Miss Price," he said, and I looked at him in surprise. "It's nice to finally meet you. I came all the way from Montana, and I can say it was entirely worth it. I never liked Texas, although my opinion of the state is quickly changing. I mean, if it has awesome people like you and Aiden and Darnell in it, how can I hate it, right?"

He droned on, talking about all kinds of things, the crickets yammering around us. I watched his lips pull up and his eyes crinkle in the corners, and I knew I would be okay. No matter what was thrown my way, as long as Cody was with me, I would survive. I might have been born in Texas and grown up in Mom's house, but I had come to learn that home wasn't a static place. It was a feeling instilled by strangers that took one into their house and lavished them with joy. It was in simple things like sharing drinks with friends and intimate moments with the person you loved. It transcended the world, reaching across continents in the form of written words.

I didn't know what my future held. I hoped Dad and Missy might one day come to accept me for who I was and who I loved. I prayed I became a better person, someone like Cody whose compassion touched many. But I had a home again and people who cared about me, and the light had never before shone so brightly.

Home was with Cody, whether we were in Montana or Texas or another country.

STERLING RIVERS lives in Chicago with their army of pets and likes to spend their days talking to the scores of hunky men in their head. When they're not writing, they like to waste time on the computer and listen to music. They hope to one day retire from their boring day job and hang out with the boys. For the latest updates, subscribe to Sterling Rivers's mailing list.

Mailing list: eepurl.com/bqb9FX
Facebook: www.facebook.com/profile.php?id=100009287517114
E-mail: Sterlingrivers3@gmail.com

Also from Dreamspinner Press

NEW LEASE OF LIFE

LILLIAN FRANCIS

www.dreamspinnerpress.com

Also from Dreamspinner Press

home for hope

RESURRECTING
HOPE

SHELL
TAYLOR

www.dreamspinnerpress.com

Also from Dreamspinner Press

SO INTO YOU
S.E. HARMON

www.dreamspinnerpress.com

Also from Dreamspinner Press

The plays that matter **don't** happen on the field...

Winter Ball

Amy Lane

www.dreamspinnerpress.com

FOR **MORE** OF THE **BEST GAY ROMANCE**

DREAMSPINNER
PRESS

dreamspinnerpress.com

www.ingramcontent.com/pod-product-compliance
Lightning Source LLC
Chambersburg PA
CBHW060057260626
47160CB00005B/1703